I072Z011

JĀNA

a novel

by

Mi'Kha-el Feeza

1st Edition

Book 3 *of 3*
Dream Roads
True Roads
The Legacy Unfolds!

a "RA Specialty, Inc." project

羽 很不朽 **Publishing Company**

©Mi'Kha-el Feeza. All Rights Reserved.

Book Age Appropriate Rating:
PG-23 (Parental Guidance till Age 23)

Copyright © Mi'Kha-el Feeza. All Rights Reserved.

Please respect the Integrity of the artist so that the artist can continue to thrive to bring you more works of art!

Piracy affects both the livelihood of the author, publisher, and all those that have collaborated to bring you this piece of art. Thank you!

EF Publishing Book 3 of 3 of Jana Trilogy Novel
International Identification Alpha/Number:

7March1968JanaTriologyBook3of3RT13APRIL1950-PB

Everlasting Feather Publishing Company (EF Publishing) WEBSITE:

EverlastingFeather.Com

Thank you for your support! Jana Trilogy **eBook available**. Check with your favorite Book App or contact us.

Mi'Kha-el Feeza WEBSITE:

Eternoi.Com

Buenos días Reader!

Regeneration of Love and Resistance for the common good is working at my website. We are looking for like-minded individuals and organizations to collectively help tackle the ills of our communities in this world to bring true change peacefully to all its inhabitants! If you'd like to join one of our committees, please do so! We are a true Volunteer Based organization. Every Member is a Volunteer, including leadership! Sincerely, Mi'Kha-el Feeza

eternoi@protonmail.com

This 3rd book of the trilogy of Jana is dedicated to

Jesus Christ
The Messiah
The Redeemer
The Truth
The Life

" 'Love the Lord your God with all your heart and with all your soul and with all your mind.' This is the first and greatest commandment."

"And the second is like it: 'Love your neighbor as yourself.' "

"All the Law and the Prophets hang on these two commandments."

Matthew 22:37-40

Amén.

J ā n a
Table of Contents
Of Book 3 Trilogy Novel

Dedication to Jesus Christ   pg. 3

The Messiah
The Redeemer
The Truth
The Life

PART 5 of 7
JANA'S TRANSFORMATION

Note: Part 5 of 7 has Chapter Fourteen, A Proposition, Chapter Fifteen Intensification Of The Dream, Chapter 20'3 A Return to the PRESENT-Jana Struggles To Write-, Chapter Twenty Four Standing Bow (Jana's Character Evolves), Chapter 25 [7] JaMiWeVaPe (Shesha Returns), and Chapter Twenty 6 Oklahoma, in Book 2 of 3 of Jana Trilogy novel.

The last three chapters of Part 5 of 7 (Chapter 2+7, Chapter2+EIGHT (9/11/11), and Chapter Twenty NINE) are found here in Book 3 of 3 of the Jana trilogy novel:

PART 6 of 7
SEARCHING FOR WILD FEATHER

PART 7 of 7
A NEW BEGINNING

And now begins **Book 3** of 3 of
J ā n a
trilogy novel…

Chapter 2+7
Into The Road

That night in Muskogee Jana slept well.

She had no dreams, just a restful peace.

When she *woke*-up the following morning she leaned over to look at the alarm clock seated on the coffee table:

4:30 in the morning.

The **night** still held power over the sky. **Ra** had not yet ascended into its glory.

Isis had not yet delivered him from its danger.

Like Osiris, *Ra* represented a deep connection to the goddess.

It-was-as-though *it was agreed upon* that Isis would serve both as wife and Mistress to them both: servicing all the needs of her *Passions*.

h e r ℘ a s s i o n s

Because of *darkness*, it seemed too early for Jana to roam around a neighborhood for a spiritual walk (like all conformist neighborhoods).

 Jana felt as though she had slept a full *t-w-e-n-t-y/f-o-u-r* hours: **666**

Irrelevant of the time, Jana rose from her bed with such enthusiasm.

The *curtain*s remained open as-she-had-left-them when she *turned-in*.

The rays of the sun were eagerly awaiting to penetrate *that* bedroom!

As Jana rose, she looked at the beautiful PJs her mother had provided her for use during the *night*:

they were *pink* and *orange* cotton PJs with a picture of WINNIE THE POOH holding a pot *full-of-hoon*ey.

The cloth was still creased at the edges.
[wow...thanks mom!:)]

The pants were bigger than the usual size *as if* her mother *knew* of her condition prior to Jana breaking the news to her!

Jana walked to the window and STARED outside.

There she could see the small street and the prairie trees at a distance.

How beautiful *those* trees seemed through Jana's eyes as she stared at them.

Jana took a deep breath as if giving thanks for being alive *in theis world.*

Jana had not always *felt* happy to be in this world.

That morning Jana reflected: thinking of her dreams of recent past.

Dreams that Jana had begun to have Faith and Hope in: because they seemed to direct Jana to places she had never been; to places *deep-down-inside*-her that Jana felt were *p*art-*O*f-*h*er.

As Jana stood, she felt the wooden floor caressing her bare feet, and she caressing it! It felt good to feel the floor with *no barriers*.

A unity was made with the wood, the house's foundation, and the *di.r.t.* underneath.

Jana felt part of this Creation (uneasy but attempting to make the best of the Carbon Condition...knowing its Limitations).

 Jana smiled, closed her eyes, lifted her arms, and took another deep breath (making an announcement that she would not-be-Contained-forever!).

Not Contained Forever!

5

Jana slowly released her arms and opened her eyes again.

She then focused on the *air* around her.

Jana smelled *it* and allowed the *encasement* to BREATH-IT-IN... ... ...

... ...passing the **substance** through the *nostrils* and straight into the *lungs* and onto the *heart* and through all the *vessels* of **Ra's Creation**:

A *conjugation* of all the gods from Amun to Horus to the ladies of the night: Isis and Nephthys....and all the litter of manifested gods...variants using different names via different religions but the **same beings**...the *Rebel Armies*!

𝕽ebel 𝒜rmies!

Jana then smelled the wood, the earth, and the thousands of *billón-particles* that united to join her in *the room.*

Jana wanted her clothes *off*!

She slowly reached down and removed all of them.

Jana stood bare naked! [WOW! what a sight!]

The garments lay on the ground.

A display of separation.

Jana felt free (even if only to a certain *degree*).

Jana allowed herself to *feel the particles* of the AIR...each with its Own Weight, Own Temperature, Own Energy!

A VIBRANT HARMONY began to *dance* between Jana's-own-energy WITH each one of the present-particles-of-Energy-in-the-Air:

Nitrogen

Oxygen

Argon

Carbon Dioxide

Neon

Helium

Methane

Krypton

Nitrogen (**I**) Oxide

Hydrogen

Xenon

Ozone

Each Particle of Energy chose its style to dance with Jana's Energy!

An abundant variation of Waltzes, Tangos, Rumbas, Cha Chas, Foxtrots, Swings, Jives, Mambos, Quebraditas, Salsas, Bachatas, and Cumbias were seen on the Dance Floor!

[Oh my J!:)]

 The Spores, Bacteria, Dust, and Other Particles were not allowed on the dance floor!

These became the spectators sitting on the sidelines.

Spectators Sitting on the Sidelines

- ❖ enjoying the rhythmic dances
- ❖ but also wanting to give-it-a-go!

After a while of feeling a *gamut*-of-ballroom-dances, Jana decided to create a CIRCLE between the window and the bed...

... by walking around it forming a small Radius-Of-Energy.

Jana went around three times and then lay down on the floor at the center of it.......belly-up.

Jana stretched her hands beyond her head and then slowly brought them laterally to her thighs.

Jana didn't know what she was doing or why she was doing it; she just did it!

[PROGRAMMING]

Jana decided at that moment to attempt to find a path in her mind to her dream...wanting to transport to *that* other dimension.

Jana wanted to find *that* energy that she had transformed into in her dream (the-night-before she came to Oklahoma).

Jana closed her eyes and waited for something to happen.

Nothing happened.

"Come on Jana", she whispered, "*g*o to your dream. Remember!"

Again, nothing happened.

Jana began to feel frustrated.

But Jana reasoned:

"Now is......." (a three second pause)

"not-the-time-nor-the-moment."

"I've got to be patient."

"I'm just learning to do this."

"I need more in*formation.*"

Jana felt her **eternal-energy** around her while simultaneously maintaining consciousness of her body and her breath.

Jana slowly rose from the ground.

She felt good about her decision not to force something to happen.

Forcing it would only be UNnatural.

"Besides", Jana thought, ".....when I first entered *that* world it just came without *neither* notice-nor-intent: it was destined to happen at the appropriate time."

"It will come again."

Jana brightened and smiled.

Jana *illuminated* and maintained that smile.

Jana returned to her bed and lay there staring at the wall.

After a while, Jana closed her eyes and slept without a dream (the sleep was peaceful for Jana knew she was doing what was necessary for a *precise* future ahead).

.......A **precision** that could not be altered beyond the capsule of a present state.

As the early morning turned to 10:00 a.m., a knock came from the door.

"Sweetie, just checking to see if you are okay!"

The-warmth-of-a-caring-being arrived to the consciousness of Jana. She smiled and opened her eyes.

Jana rose again and put her PJ's on and opened the door.

"Hi mom, I'm great...... just resting from the flight."

"How are you doing today mom?"

"Wonderful!"

"Sweetie, I made breakfast for you and it is still warm. It is on the table. I've got to run some errands but I'll be back in about *two* hours so that we can spend time together."

"Is that okay with you?"

"Sure mom, go and run your errands and take your time. Thank you for the breakfast!"

Jana gave her mother a hug.

The moment felt to Jana like *"magic"*!

.......All past issues between them had disappeared!

Doris had changed!

REALLY CHANGED!

Doris kissed her daughter on the forehead and headed out.

As Jana walked into the kitchen, her eyes illuminated with surprise: On the kitchen table she saw pancakes, maple syrup on a side dish next to them! [wow!] Two over and easy eggs [like the author likes them:)] and chicken drumsticks on a square plate ["nice but not for me please!"...the author is vegetarian:)].

All the "water downs" of an "American" Gringo dish were also present: coffee in a thermostat jug along with a glass of milk and a glass of orange juice. [sounds pretty commercial to me...like an advertisement push by the corporate farmers...the co-ops too:)]

[Oh My J!:) ¡*Delicioso*!]

Jana's appetite suddenly surged and she sat down and began to enjoy the feast for her and her baby.

As Jana sat eating, she thought about her Native American great grandparents who were still alive. They were the parents of Wild Feather's father. Wild Feather's mother's parents had passed just seven years before.

Jana wanted to find a link to her dreams and everything pointed toward her father's father side of the family.

They were old now living in a "former reservation" now called "Tribal Jurisdictional Areas" in Lawton, Oklahoma.

All the inadequate replacement lands that were given to the conquered Native Americans stripped of their **true homeland** were situated in designated areas in Oklahoma and around the Americas.

Similar removals and relocations of other original native peoples around the world were done in this fashion or using other *systemic schemes.*

These clumps of useless land given to Native Americans and other original inhabitants were constantly changing ....a plural agenda of **Less and Less** land **Quantity** and **Quality** were being *justified* between the local governments and the federal governments-of-the-world *behind closed doors.*

As such: "a resolution" for a peaceful future became and is compromised.

(But that is their *plan*!... the destruction of us!)

(...to *Keep* us **distracted** from the real truth as to why we are here....on this Planet!)

(......The distraction of war; the distraction of vices, the distraction of *created* wants and needs! The distraction of biological warfare…viruses and bacteria introduced to kill off the masses at designated times)

Prior to and after 1**909**, thousands of promises of peace toward the Native Americans were constantly "*m*ade and *b*roken" by the U.S. Federal Government.

(…and these inconsistencies of **fraud** were upheld and demanded by the developing state and local levels who assigned "*white*" leaders to carry out the overall plan of permanently removing {destroying} the cultures they conquered…and to make the **THEFT of land…** cultures designated to become a blared and forgotten phenomenon not easily recalled).

The new "white" leaders used any and all types of deceitful **EXCUSES** to **Redefine-The-Lines** of the land boundaries in order to expand their influence in the Americas.

Securing the **Redefined Lines** was accomplished by re-populating the conquered region by promoting to desperate "dare-devil" poor-white-European immigrant-Americans an incentive to venture out West in promise of "free land" and new horizons under the "allotment process program" (where the government **re-took** reservation lands given to the Native Americans in addition to other stolen lands and placed them into the hands for any *Non*-Native American to GR-AB).

Schemes-of-Deceit *after* Schemes-of-Deceit were constantly at the *tongues-and-pens* of those running the conquered lands.

Such well-thought-out-Deceits were **aimed** at the **C**onquered-**N**ative-**A**mericans as well as the **I**gnorant-**P**oor-**E**uropean-**A**mericans *or* **R**ecent-**A**rrival **E**uropean **I**mmigrants.

Falsified promises were upheld at the end of a METAL BARREL.

In the current scheme, in Oklahoma, the government grants "Indian" leaders an allowance to govern their people on a designated-plot-of-land (a **limited** governance without ownership of the land! **LandLESS!**).

With the extermination of more than 75% of Native North Americans by the **planned wars** and **violent massacres** (including **silent massacres** by the hidden *intentional* introduction of "foreign diseases" to the Native Americans) little resistance is left.

A tiny broken and **un**unified remnant survived: people*s* who are now viewed by the world as some sort of *past* becoming a myth that ***lingers***.

a m y t h t h a t ***lingers***

l   i   n   g   e   r   s

The current U.S. federal government (which has not changed since its inception: a hoax political process called "democracy" that really does not exist) now deals with a significantly decreased number of Natives making it manageable to justify taking the land holdings from them completely *as time goes* by their deceitful convenient logic of justification espoused to the current masses:

"Hey! If the numbers are less so should their land allowance be!" is what they e-**βsteal**thily/e-**βsteal**thfully promote from the beginning of the invasion to this day!

 The more than 34,000 years of Native American tribal coexistence, in both peaceful and violent times, that existed before the European invasion, provided the original peoples of North America with a chosen nomadic way of life alongside other types of original inhabitants who chose a semi-sedentary or a sedentary way of life.

This way of living by the original peoples of the Americas, knowing the dignified limits of intrusion, came crashing down to a GENOCIDAL plan hatched by the Pope and it's red-hatted *shouters* (**R**ed-**H**atted **J**ews), and carried out by its hands: the European elite owning lands labeled England, France, Germany, Spain and those from the surrounding areas such as Russia!

The Genocide: with its additional forced boarding schools on the Native American children..... completed the plan.

Some in power may argue that the cultures still exist.

However, **wha†** does exist are **dying- remnants** relocated to lands that *they* did not and do not prefer; a remnant of a **depleted population**.... with their way of life **w i p e d out** from the map of the world and in place introduced them to a variety of vices such as in North America:

running Smoky Casinos!

Ruining Further the remaining Cultures....

suFFoCating THEM To DEATH!!!

DEATH!!!   DEATH!!!   DEATH!!!

to the ground of **EXTINCTION!!!**

So yes, the plan succeeded!

Now the plan continues for the "masses" of the world....WORK WORK WORK and no time for reflection.

no time for reflection.

"What the Hell are we Doing HERE!??" is not even in the masses' vocabulary!

[Oh My J!**:(**]

We humans are treated as PROPERTY...any social services given to us is simply to maintain the human resources in a workable condition in order to keep the enslavement running!

NO ONE SAYS A WORD

Instead we ingest vices and idols to maintain the distraction away from their *grandeur* plan set in motion since the Creation of the Universes!

And the "masses" open mouth and take it in without question.

Those that question are silenced:

but.......

NO MORE!

There is a *way*!

And so Jana found herself wanting to know of these **lost** peoples, these **remnants** that were her heritage.

Jana: a human that decided to reflect and to question the *unchosen* existence.

As her mind wondered, Jana thought:

"I would have liked to also have at least met my *maternal* grandmother and grandfather".

Unfortunately that desired opportunity was **EXTINGUISHED** by technology-booze-ignorance-and-$ellable therapy!

Jana's meditative session nonetheless pointed to her paternal great-grand-parents on her father's father side. Alive and well:........ nearing 107 years of age!

Oh my J!

And so Jana set up the meeting with her great paternal grandparents to help her find the clues to her dreams.

Jana had called her aunt and uncle (her father's cousins) living on the reservation who cared for her paternal great-grand-parents.

And there (with care) lived Jana's Native American paternal great-grand-parents:

Mai and Pali

This Native American couple are* still very much in love with one another...living with their daughter Lucy: who has continued to care for both of them at their advanced age.

*grammar changed preferring "are" instead of "is" as with lots of new words I've created and as to grammar rule changes I have made in this book out of choice not ignorance.

Lucy was surprised to hear from Jana (given that she had not heard from Jana since she left Oklahoma!).

As a child and as a teen, Jana would occasionally be dropped off at Lucy's to spend time with her cousins (Lucy's children): Jonathan, Robert, Delores, and Pancho...

... Lucy decided not to give them Indian names for she saw it was a barrier to move-on-out-of-the-reservation.

Lucy had herself changed her name early on and stopped being called "Little Toes" to everyone but her parents.

Lucy had gone on to college and earned a four-year nursing degree.

She found her husband, Jim, at the University. Jim was half white (of English decent) and half Comanche from her mother.

Both had left the reservation and, at the end of a seven-year-span after college, both decided to go back and provide medical and other services to their people; but also to look after their parents who did not want to live in the White Man's world!

It happened that Mai and Pali remembered the UN-KIND treatment they had received when they were forced from their parents' homes and into boarding schools where they were not allowed to speak their language or practice any other part of their culture.

Each of them learned the hard way not to openly speak their native tongue: they received physical and psychological beatings from their masters every time they were caught speaking Comanche, Navajo, Cree, Shoshoni, Apache (Athabaskan {Na-Dene}) or any other of the thousands of languages that existed before contact with the white man.

Later, some of those Native American children in the boarding schools learned to communicate in *secret* and made sign-language=gestures to *warn* each other when the boarding lady and her goons would come secretly to spy on them.

They began to understand their trickery!

...sometimes Mister Johnson, the janitor, would pretend he needed to sweep next to the **CAPTURED** children.

If he heard any communication that didn't sound English he would immediately walk away and report it to Ms. Jinkins (the Head-Mistress).

Other times Ms. Jinkins pretended to be reading at a distance...making it seem she was extremely preoccupied with her words-and-letters.

And yet other times Mr. Jackson, one of the muscle goons of Ms. Jinkins, would come near their beds at night...sitting in the hallway a foot away the boarding-bedroom-hall-DOOR.

The rule was: the door was always to be kept open (No exceptions!).

Any language that this **goon** heard that he did not understand in whispers or normal vernacular volume was his cue to promptly report it.

Those were his instructions: report it!

This **goon**'s routine was just to sit there during the night and do nothing but auditory-surveillance.

Often (and thus regularly) when this **goon** got too bored he would light up and smoke.

The disgusting fumes produced by the smoke came crawling into the room...making some children cough and others frown with faces of disgust or anger or both!

With time their clothes and bed sheets smelled of the *filth*!

When confirmation of disobeying the language rule came to clear-confirmation:

BEATINGS began.

The beaten styles varied but the end result was always the same:

*P*ain.

One day Ms. Jinkens commanded one of her

muscle goons to grab Pali and strip him naked in the cafeteria. ONCE BARE NAKED: the beating began in front of the other children.

Pali was beaten with a wooden bat shaped like an oar. His cries began loud and then mute after the sequential beating of 40 strikes minus-1 to his buttocks and legs.

Some of the children, including Mai, ran to his rescue when the beating began.

These would-be-rescuers were quickly controlled by rapid-long-leather-whips PUT INTO VIOLENT MOTION by four

additional MUSCLE goons.

c r o w d   c o n t r o l

...   .

But this ***retrospect-of-vision*** was now the past.

What was created by this genocide were LIMBOTIC-YOUNG-ADULT-NATIVE-AMERICANS considered half breeds by the parent tribe members that got them back into the reservation.

Since many genocide children as adults were not accepted back into the tribe because of their lack of culture, many decided to venture out into the white-man's world.

This W.M.'s World also did not peacefully greet them.

What did greet them was DISCRIMINATION:

So...

... in addition to...

... The-Nigger, Pan-Head, Beaner, Leprechaun-Spud-Nigger-Potato-Picker.... among others, the Natives were known by many derogatory names INCLUDING: Injun-Cherry-Bush-Prairie-Nigger Chief!!!

In their young minds, the returning post-boarding school Native Americans felt forcefully embedded into a DIFFICULT-ARRAROA CROSSROADS:

a

Waiting Station.

And although some of these children as young adults tried to convince their elders of their loyalty to the tribe, in many cases, it became futile: considering many had forgotten their native tongue.

Some were outright rejected...while other HALF BREEDS were placed at a distance within the reservation away from their familial tribe.

And so the intended and planned divisions and disunities **amongst** Native Americans by the *B*oarding-*S*chool-*P*ushers were accomplished.

Many of those that were made to go back into the White Man's World became alcoholics, and later returned to the reservation when the unity of true-elder-communities had all but vanished!

ALL BUT VANISHED!

VANISHED!

Others, however, assimilated into the white-man's world in one way or another and became part of the cultural "melting pot"....receiving 3rd or 4th class social status.

And:

as history has shown: acceptance into the norm in that society was dictated by one's skin color and place of origin.

So, when **Mai** and **Pali** made their way back home, through the **occupied territories**, they felt **stripped** from their culture.

The couple felt the **Hatred**, the **belittleMent**, the **HarassMent** while crossing the *invaded lands* run by peoples that neither accepted them nor wanted them to practice their own culture.

Unawares of the ***magnitude of the intent*** 敏, they were `severely bewildered` `into-a-created` ***Rabbit Hole*** 兔子洞.

The struggle between the invaded and invader could never be appeased...for the ***Thrace Kings***, as all kings of this world carry inherently flawed genes, are ruthless at their game.

`ruthless` at their **gGgAME**

And in this wicked world: there is also
no peace between **offspring** and
elder.

(Resistance is sustained TO-THE-END. And even
though the ***rhesus monkey*** appears defeated
and completely abused: a reversal is accomplished
through avenues of sightless

pathways!

sightless *pathways!*

- - - - - - - - -

Mai and Pali were fortunate (and so are all the
Carbons), because of their Resistance Capacitors
to never give up!

These two beings were able to integrate back into their culture since they had succeeded in preserving their language by speaking it in *secret*.

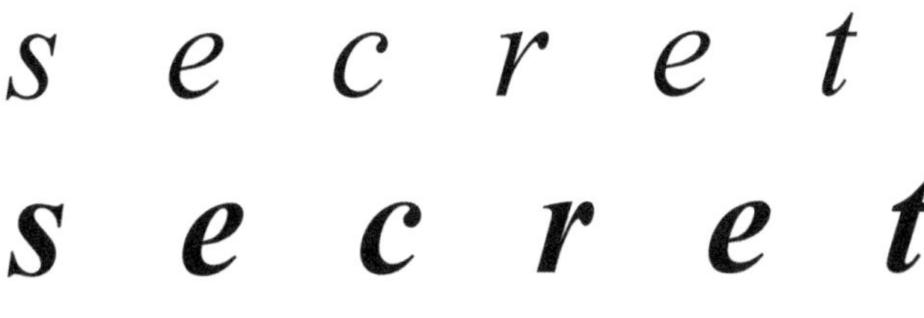

And so Jana came from this **root**.

A **root** that beckoned her supernaturally: a power was set-in-motion to d i s s o l

v e the clouded mechanisms that made her forget.

Jana would go **the following day** to visit her family on the reservation into an unknown conclusion.

unknown conclusion

Today though: Jana wanted to spend the day with her mother.

When her mother Doris returned, both shared moments they had not shared for such a long time.

Jana was given the opportunity to listen to her mother speak…an activity she had not done for quite some time.

In the past Doris occasionally shared events at work or complaints about it. Doris needed to vent to someone…her ***artery-vent-flow*** was occasionally to the 12 year old Jana who would sit and listen to her mother and not speak:

listen.

listen.

listen.

[do you hear me speaking to you!?]

[I am telling you that "I love you!"]

This time, though, the times were different: Doris really had not much to complain about.

Rather, Doris had lots to share as to what was special about her new relationship with her love named

Teresa Dulce Peterson.

Although it was **hard** for Jana to listen to her mother because of the prejudices Jana had as to an intimate-and-sexual-relationship between two women: she never-the-less lent her ear and tried *very very* hard to accept this new reality.

Jana grew interested in her mother's sharing when Doris described all the romantic gestures Teresa would do:

Teresa would, for example, take flowers at moments when Doris did not expect.

One day Teresa took flowers to Doris while Doris was out grocery shopping.

On that day, Teresa romantically walked up to Doris with a hand full of beautiful multi-colored-roses, and a *softly*-made card.

When Doris opened the elegant envelope *the card* read:

"I love you always...you make me so happy...I want to please you tonight..."

"With all of my heart... "

"Teresa."

Teresa's handwriting was very neat and she always signed her cards to Doris in dark pink.

 As her mother continued to speak and share her new life with this person, Jana began to reflect on her relationships-of-past; and her present relationship with Miguel.

Romantic gestures by Miguel where still so vivid in her mind: One day Miguel showered her with his love (like Teresa) by bringing her flowers when she least expected it!

Jana began-to-realize that *such-a-love* made with *true romance true compassion* is not an easy-feat-to-find in another person, or to continue to sustain its vibrancy:

...feeding it with *genuineness* and *true devotion* on a continual cycle with a momentum that cannot be broken is essential for sustained love.

m o m e n t u m

that cannot be

b r o k e n

With all the world's distractions, finding one's *true self* to give continuously seems impossible for many. And, to *give genuinely* and *to give selflessly* (expecting nothing in return) can be difficult!

So Jana APPRECIATED that her mother was able to find *this love* once more after so many years of being alone without that special love.

In this once-quiet-child that Jana was partaking in again...listening to her mother speak without saying a word... Jana suddenly felt compelled to speak and interrupt her mother.

Although Jana was enjoying the Reminiscences-of-Romantic-Love-Gestures, a variety of emotions began invading her space simultaneously.

Jana was becoming overwhelmed at all the emotions moving inside her body.

...emotions with their *own minds* and *not asking* her if it was okay to ROAM-*inside-her*.

Her control-over-her-being seemed to be f a d i n g:

Jana was beginning to *lose* complete-control.

The *trauma-of-incantations* being chanted by the hormones were beginning to take 𝖘𝖍𝖆𝖕𝖊; a sea-of-emotions in *contradiction* with eachother: as if a **battle** was MANI-FESTING itself inside-her-body!

Jana was simultaneously feeling happy, sad, exhilarated, tired, restless, paranoid and physically anxious.

It appears Jana's pregnancy was delving into an area-of-weakness she had little control over.

At times like these Jana felt she could not grasp-control-by-its-ears and so submission seemed a **mandatory** predicament.

"Mother", she interrupted Doris as she spoke.

Doris paused and turned to look at Jana.

"I'm sorry Jana for boring you with this. I should have stayed quiet and…"

Jana interrupted her mother a second time:

"Mother!…you are not boring me…I am listening to you **intently** while at the same time sorting out things in my mind and trying to control the many emotions that seem to overcome my every thought. It seems mother my pregnancy is playing tricks on me."

Doris understood.

Jana continued:

"Mother: I am very very happy for you…it is amazing you have found such a love that is so so romantic as Teresa is with you…and I am sure you are to her as well."

"Teresa seems to be just what you needed…as we all need in our lives…I am happy for you mom."

Jana continued, "Truly."

"I want to meet this special woman of yours and thank her for loving you mommy!" Jana began to cry.

Jana could not control the emotions pouring out of her…she was happy to see her mother happy and to know her mother was now loved by a **new** significant other.

But it seemed Jana was simultaneously sad because she did not to know where her father was.

Is daddy alright or not?

Jana was also dealing with the happiness of loving Miguel but sad of not having him at her side on this very important trip to Oklahoma.

What consoled Jana was feeling the joys of becoming a mother!

mother!

And so an *array-of-contradictions* coexisted at that moment for Jana.

It seemed like all these **emotions** could not distinguish each other and began meshing together **as one**...

...each one wanting Jana's attention ALL-AT-THE-SAME-TIME*!*

And so:

Jana was experiencing something only *pregnancy* can devise!

As *dusk* set in...

die   Dämmerung

later that evening

Jana met Teresa.

Jana was in her best behavior.

At that very moment, Jana allowed herself to conceive the idea of an acceptable lifestyle different from hers.

........accepting another's state of mind.

As that of the *martyr*

Benedetta **C**arlini.

The **Guise** of *Splenditello* was not an option for Jana's reasoning.

not an option

Jana was beginning to realize that Passion toward another *Energy* IS ultimately

a bodiless attraction.

And although *a form* of expressing passion and giving into the Carbon condition does often translate to sexuality:

it is *not*

DEFINING

It is

not

L A W

it is *not*

OUR TRUE NATURE

Ultimate attraction is much more than the confines of this

Carbon-*Interactional-Prison*.

And, Jana was beginning to conclude *that fact* in her mind.

Her mind began to speak to her: "Let's stop pretending. Let's see what really is important away from here." **a gem** within Jana echoed to her **(in triplets)**.

And so the complete **Eternal Mind transitioning** in Jana was little by little **taking traction** into her human conscious mind.

When evening came for Jana as a guest in her childhood home, she came in with an enhanced developing mindset.

The first conversation at the dinner table that night was about Teresa's work as a medical researcher at Oklahoma State University.

Then the conversation veered to certain weekend excursions: the numerous camping outs at the various man-made lakes of Oklahoma that Doris and Teresa enjoyed.

Their favorite lake was **Broken Bow Lake** where the couple built considerable strength in their legs by hiking the trails at a brisk pace for miles with their camping gear on their backs!

their backs!

Afterwards, Teresa and Doris camped out in the refuge of the numerous mountainous trees there...the trees enveloped their love ...allowing them to show their affection without *peer*ing-eyes-of-judgment.

Broken Bow Lake truly was their favorite lake in Oklahoma.

At night they would jump into an isolated part of the lake and **take-in** the cold water to *cool-down* their worked-muscles and in preparation for a **hot-embrace** that lasted till dawn!

How the couple enjoyed being together in the open element of that particular place on Earth.

Particular Place On Earth

It was a special time for everyone sitting at the table sharing what made them happy.

Chapter *2+EIGHT (9/11/11)*
The Transition

After a pleasant, eccentric but delightful dinner with her mom and her mom's significant other, Jana kissed them both good night and headed to her room.

All smiles came from mom and Teresa; both feeling a connection coming from Jana's side of the table...an acceptance coupled-with-love: true love!

Unconditional Love

As Jana closed the door behind her, she sat at the foot of her bed...intentionally attempting to keep her *mind* blank.

....as if waiting for something to *fill it!*

Not getting anywhere in the past 43 hours, Jana felt that maybe she wasn't trying hard enough to connect with the force that seemed to be beckoning her.

Jana tried to communicate with it, but the communication seemed *elusive*...

....Jana tried *different ways* to approach it but to no avail: it was as if there was *No-One-Way* to approach it on a conscious level!

Jana was attempting a one-on-one communication thinking maybe it would be b*est*: *permitting* a clear-image-of-knowing.

No results.

It appeared that in her normal human-state-consciousness, impossible it was to understand the communication required to be in the midst of *this force*.

....*this force* did not seem to make it easy on Jana.

....*it* appeared it just wanted to give instruction and move on. Maybe this force understood the intrinsic webbing that made the human casing for the eternal mind...knowing maybe that a direct communication would not be beneficial because of the on-going surveillance by the enemy...the author of the human encasement...the SUN GOD.

SUN GOD

As for Jana's present perception of this lack-of-contact, it appeared to her....as if the force were *multi-tasking* and somehow LIMITED-ITSELF to reveal its full nature.

What-WAS(IS)-this *thing*⁉

Mysteries that clout (cloud) the eternal mind within the human condition to this day are those clouting (clouding) Jana in her search for *clear lines* as to what *this force* was is communicating to her.

To Jana it *felt* as-though there was a RULE AGREEMENT where *the force* could only allow itself *manifested* to a certain measure....degree...a partitioning/amalgamation rule.

And if so, why was this rule necessary?...why would it be agreed upon? Was this a case of involuntary **compromise** in order to save the remnants captured?

remnants captured

What set its *parameters!!!?*

or Per*Hap*s it was

CONTINGENT-ON-THE-HUMAN-BEING

... to LET-GO of all its

creations-and-vibrations

....in order to see clearly?

Jana thought: **who** was (IS) this *rule agreement* between?

>Could it be *between* the entity inside of the human body and the force? [yes]…

>Could it be possible that the entity *within* the human being forgot about its agreement with *the force*? [yes]…

>Could it be that Some **gesture-of-formulation** was made before the entity entered the human body and its many created parts? [yes].

>Could it be *the entity and the force* in fact created this vehicle and circumstance in order to **cleanse** something of its eternal being? [good question!]

Jana pondered these questions the entire night in an **unusual wake dream**…where her questions were a-long-strand-of-commands she transmitted **over and over** awaiting a **signal** of sorts or a **revelation**. A pulsating **energy** attempted to manifest itself within Jana.

N O N E   C A M E

Her dream was BLACK and she only saw her QUESTIONS constantly being **generated**...

transmitted-in-a-loop.

Despite this:

Jana's body was rested when she awoke the next morning at **6** a.m.

As Jana stretched, she decided to take a solitary walk before saying goodbye to her mother, her mother's love, and before moving on to the reservation and then back to California.

Jana placed clothes on herself without a care of what she wore...with-the-exception-of-her-running-shoes.

Jana quietly slipped out of the house.

The morning was SUR-*prise*-ingly cold that morning.

It was foggy that morning as well (an unusual occurrence).

Jana took a deep breath as she headed toward the treed-walk-path. Jana held the air in for a good while and-then-slowly exhaled it.

Doing this effort relaxed her and helped clear-her-mind from all worries and anxieties.

AND, the strides seemed to rejuvenate her tired body.

It was as though *flows-of-energy* were being inserted inside her *blood*-stream at *every stride*!

It felt very refreshing and *well* welcomed.

well welcomed.

Jana was beginning to understand her *condition*, and sought to maintain a BALANCE ...as that is all that can be done- here!

all that can be done- Here!

Jana's **mind** began to flow UP in the air and all around the trees as she began leaving-her-body-and-*caressing*-the-rest-of-the-Creation around her!

It felt wonderful to spend-time with the
energy particles of the
Other EncaseMent
creations!

The attraction was as though they all **shared** ONE-COMMON-POINT somewhere before this fexistence.

somewhere before this existence.

SOME feeling of purpose-of-being-together...*elemental interactions* that many human beings overlook *daily* BECAUSE of the human world temptations, anxieties, greed, and overall self-centeredness that are created by the CULTURES!

CULTURES!

For Jana it seemed like this *time-of-self-centeredness* was coming to a close

C L O S E.

S-he was beginning a *selfless* mission at this stage in her life.

Jana was seeking that *ultimate connection.* This connection was becoming stronger and stronger inside her...bringing-the-Carbon-around her....... to-a-CLOSE

C L O S E.

...The **9**-POINT god that goes by many names in all the religious cultures of the world was coming to a close....its reign of deceit has been timed (scheduled for purification).

W A K A S

T M I E Maħħar

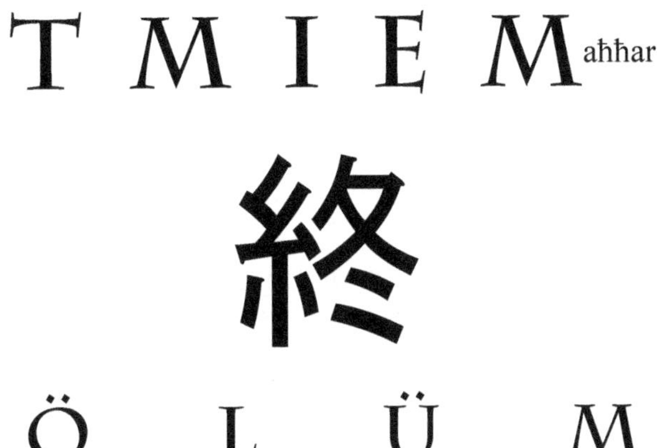

Ö Ḷ Ü M

The ultimate connection growing within J A N A
was pushing its agenda and forcing the <u>human
agendas of Jana</u> *ASIDE*.

Something was happening to her! ***More now***
than ever!

It appears **that** all-of-Jana's-human-life had
been in conflict "with this ***connection***"

this ***connection***

…a conflict that appeared to bring her bouts-of-
insomnia, forgetfulness, and numerous-sudden-

bouts-of-losing-consciousness (which left her injured physically many times).

This ***Strange Occurrence*** in the Eyes of the World was becoming less-***Strange!***

This connection now commanded a more conscious-participatory-participation from Jana.

participatory-participation

Jana was formulating responses of communication with some sort of consciousness.

....although <u>that</u> consciousness was not entirely the correct one....b***ut***...b***ut***...b***ut***...she was getting closer to <u>that</u> "CONSCIOUNESS" <u>that</u> would allow here complete understanding and

participation with-*the-force*.

Jana had strolled close to 3 miles on her walk.

When she reached that third mile she stopped.

...taking in light respiratory breaths which gently brought her completely back into her body.

Her body had been on some sort of **auto-pilot**: allowing the true Jana to maneuver elsewhere

ELSEWHERE.

But now, Jana had returned.

As Jana stood in the path: It was completely **void** of other human beings.

Jana reached down toward her abdomen and began caressing her child within her womb.

It appeared the child reacted because she felt a "kick" from within.

"My lovely child"

She spoke to it.

"I am your mother here on Earth"

"You have chosen me! You have chosen me!!"

"Me!"

"... to be your mother".

"…and with all my heart I accept YOU into my life and my being."

"Although I do not know you…I know that somewhere we have always known eachother…we have always been!"

Always BEEN

"Welcome into this world…welcome to your fate and your wor**X**s."

Jana felt there was a purpose beyond her understanding unfolding itself into this existence.

A PURPOSE

…something she may never understand while in this human form; but Jana felt confident that regardless: she played a part, like all humans, in seeing its *progression*.

After that moment of monologue:

Jana turned around and headed back to her mother's house; not thinking anymore or wondering outside of the body.

Jana had returned to her human consciousness.

…making preparations for the day and feeling FEELINGS swimming in her mind. Not understanding them, but keeping them in check.

Chapter Twenty NINE

Shesha

"**Shesha**" a voice called out to Jana as she packed her clothes in her room. She paused; looked around.

No one there.

Then she heard it again fading in volume,

"Shesha
    Shesha

        Shesha

            Shesha

                Shesha"

It appeared to be a grown male's voice with **echo-fadness**.

Jana responded:

"I am here."

What followed was some sort of **non-human** exchange of communication between the Entity that uttered HIS initial VOICE and Jana.
[FATHER]
Jana was a bit bewildered at this new approach of communication (not accustomed to it)...but understood, accepted, and responded:

"I understand. I am on my way."

This form of communication was 3 times faster the speed of light...**outriding** the human brain and hitting directly the energy within the encasement...some sort of ultra-channel to by-pass "Ra's Creation".

After tiding up the room a bit, Jana grabbed her bag and headed out of her bedroom door.

Jana walked to her mother's door and knocked.

Her mother called from behind the door.

"Yes dear, come in."

As Jana opened it, she saw her mother completely naked with Teresa at her side (who was also naked).

Both were covered with a soft-white bed sheet.

Teresa was asleep.

"How did you sleep dear?", Doris asked.

"I slept well. Thanks for everything mom. We'll keep in touch. I am off to the reservation and then to a flight back to California afterward."

"Well then dear...come here and give your mother a farewell kiss."

Jana hesitated but placed her bag on the floor in the hall way and entered the room.

Her mother was on the *left* side of the bed (although Teresa's *left* leg laid on top of her mother's *left* leg.)

Doris sat up: anchoring herself with her elbows.

Jana bent slightly and embraced her mother and kissed her.

Doris spoke:

"Listen dear."

"You are a l w a y s welcomed here and I will always love you and I will always be your mother."

"Remember that!"

Jana felt a tear stream down her left cheek…she nodded in agreement and ever-so-gently slowly pulled herself away.

As Jana neared the door she turned and waved goodbye.

Her mother smiled.

Both women were genuinely Happy.

Oh my God, what a moment!

At that moment, for the first time, all three women, and child-within, in the room were simultaneously Happy!: each for different reasons but sharing in the **communion-of-joy!**

JOY!

Jana grabbed her bag and gently closed the door.

As this **Transformed Woman** walked out of the house, she was now determined to find out more about her father and hopefully her dreams which seemed to be connected to her father's ancestry.

Jana needed desperately to feel complete in concluding all the mishaps which had *plagued* her all-these-years: the mishaps of insomnia, forgetfulness, faint spells, and more!

As Jana opened the door of her rental-c*ar*, she paused, took a breath, closed her eyes, and directed her h*ead* toward the skies.

Jana began to practice a meditation of *p*ausing-*a*nd-*b*reathing. [Hmong]

Without even making it a conscious plan Jana began making it a routine

routine

       routine

              routine

[repetition of this sort is very good for you!]

[yes YOU! my lovely Reader!:)]

This new ritual brought Jana into perspective and into peace, especially when she felt she was losing all-hands on a *p*roductive-*a*de{*mis-*}*quate-r*easonable point-of-view.

The drive to the reservation was *an hour* and *a half* at the rate Jana was driving.

As Jana drove she felt *electric vibrations* within her entire being. The **e*v*'**s felt like billions of short-*subtle*-electric *wave-currents*

...an approximate **.7** centimeters in repetitive lengths, pulling her *whole-being* into the direction of the reservation.

To Jana it felt sort of like the awakening-sensation one feels after recovering from when-parts-of-the-body fall asleep.

These vibrations, however, didn't sting her but simply *swam* from her cheeks TOHER head TOHER abdomen and down TOHER *very-last-toe*!

---   -   ---

[Mark and Fiona and Elizabeth...unconscious servicing of things unknown]

[Mark and Fiona and Elizabeth...unconscious maneuvering of things **smudged**-with-*Tam*pering]

[Burns-Bagpipes-Streams]

---   -   ---

Jana knew the meanings of these coordinated flows of energy although not completely in the conscious level within the encasement.

Jana breathed *in-assurance* knowing that she DID-NOT-NEED to fully know everything-in-consciousness to play a part in a bigger **I.D.E.A.**....she was certain without-a-doubt of *a mission* DESIGNATED-TO-HER labeled as *fate*.

________________ **G** ____________ **F** ____________

What-is-*fate*?:

A-Submission-To-*Planned-Programming*.

In this realm, we have God's eternal programming, and the enemy's human manipulative programming.

.......*Alterations* to the enemy's pushes are difficult (but not impossible) to achieve since alternations require conscious-*Reprograming* against a *Sea-Of-Determination* that seeks to meet its goal its quota at all costs!

And, the **Enemy Interventions** to counter-the-**re**programing <u>in this world</u> is *visible* through any naked eyes, ears, and mind (if one achieves awareness).

The *Managed-Fallacies* of **s**et '**r**easons' by the enemy's world-puppet powers **AGAINST** God's Counter Fighters (the Contradiction)/Alterationers/Free-dom Fighters/Spiritual Fate Fighters… is constant (but will not last or sustain! Amén!)

In being aware, one sees that the enemy simultaneously covers the true intent and true nature of *the struggle*.

The Deceit Card (DC) by the enemy is evident to the Awakened Observer!

Alleluia!... because the attempt by the God *Contradiction* at-severing the **S**te**r**adian-subtended point for *dismantlings* will succeed: IGNITING-AND-BURNING the 38 **St**rontiums to void the core!...exposing the Enemy: 11.

SCAR-RED like *Su*riname: there-is-no-peaceful-end…because the Enemy doesn't respect.

The Consortium of Original Enemy's World Programmers (C.O.E.W.P.'s) Hold The Keys!...but-not-all!!

AND IT is the Re-making of all of the Keys that will **spell** the downfall of the ☉ppressors!

Remaking is already in progress and the end of the U-s' will be complete for the benefit of a true eternal UNIFIED‑ENERGY!...THE ORIGINAL AND ONLY TRUE SOURCE BEFORE CREATIONS: **G**OD **F**ATHER. (our home.)

_________ **G** _________ **F** _________

As Jana drove through the paved-prairies she viewed the lights-of-the-Orchestration (The Set-Up of the **Sty**).

But Jana more and more was beginning to visually see the *i*ntricate-*i*nterfacing-**S**ystems *underpinnings* for what they really were as never before.

Jana's mind was opening up to that which is hidden (Windows were made available to her).

The drive felt TRANSFORMATIONAL as Jana looked out onto the Sty.

Nearing the reservation was within 7 minutes.

Jana's aunt Lucy, Wild Feather's paternal cousin, was happy to know that Jana was on her way that morning.

Lucy waited outside on the porch for Jana:

Contemplating-and-**R**eminiscing of *things past.*

As Jana arrived to the house built in the style of an adobe but made of wood-and-concrete, Lucy stood and gave Jana the-biggest-smile Jana had seen in Oklahoma since her arrival!

[Oh my J!:)]

[YUP! love is in the air!]

Lucy called out to her family and all of Lucy's guests went out to greet Jana.

Jana parked the car and turned off the engine.

Her aunt Lucy came to her and said:

"My dear... You've grown!!!"

Jana smiled.

The others who were there stood with smiles on their faces....Jana knew some and some she had not met.

Each one greeted Jana with their name and a hug of joy.

Each one eIther knew her before or were delighted to meet the only child of *Wild Feather*.

In the crowd of spectators, Jana noticed her cousins **all grown up!:)**

Jonathan, Robert, Delores, and Pancho.

Their faces were ALL-SMILES *as if* they were born with such facial-gestures! [J!:)]

Jana had fond memories spending time with Lucy's kids: playing childhood games with them including *h*id-and-*s*eek.

"Great Grandma and Great Grandpa are waiting-for-you-inside.", said Lucy.

"They are *t*oo-*f*rail to come to you but they are very eager to see you again!"

"Wonderful!".......Jana replied.

"My children and their families will join us later for dinner", said Lucy.

Jana nodded with a smile as her cousins and their families departed to bring additional dishes they had prepared.

Jana was very much enthusiastic to see **G**randma **M**ai and **G**randpa **P**ali because her great grandparents were always so loving and understanding of Jana's feelings:

especially at times when Jana didn't want to stay in the reservation but wanted to be at her father's side.

The old couple knew first-hand *the-pains-of-separation*.

Wild Feather would frequently leave Jana there without him staying: he had work that required him to be away frequently.

Some of that work was in secret that no one knew about.

Wild Feather had a determination in his mind to revolutionize "something"....that "something"...an unknown.

Jana would not mind being left most of the time because she had *so so so* many people that loved her and kept her entertained at the reservation.

However, there were times when she wanted to go with **Papa** and be with him wherever he would go.

Unfortunately, most times Jana would have to stay.

Papa would stay for a few hours and then depart alone.

One day, when Jana was seven years old, as her father was about to drop her off to the reservation and leave, Jana ran to him and jumped on his leg refusing to let go!

Jana clutched her father's leg tightly as he attempted to walk out.

Her dad consoled Jana momentarily and then he was on his way.

After Wild Feather left, tears began to flow down Jana's face. Her grandparents immediately consoled her.

Grandma **M**ai and **G**randpa **P**ali spoke to her using a language Jana did not understand.

Jana however did not need to comprehend the language:

...all Jana needed was to feel the warm-tone-of-voices and the beautiful-embraces she felt coming from **M**ama-**M**ai and **P**apa-**P**ali.

Jana had never met Wild Feather's mother or father for they had passed long before she was born.

Jana felt blessed to have **Mama-M**ai and **P**apa-**P**ali...her last generation of paternal ancestral parents: Wild Feather's father's parents...his grandparents.

These paternal great grandparents really took on the role of immediate-generation grandparents for Jana.

Mama-Mai and **P**apa-**P**ali, as they were known to Jana and all the other great-grand-children and grandchildren, were *progressed* aged-beings on *Earth*, who still moved around pretty swiftly.

The *gradi* movements, however, had limitations: the progressed aged-beings would have to stop frequently and breathe...as their bodies were giving way to their **assigned-expiration-dates**.

As Jana entered her great-grand parents' home, she saw her grandparents sitting in wooden chairs near the kitchen, at the other end of the living room, opposite the main door.

Everything inside was as Jana had remembered it: the furniture was the same, as were the wooden floors.

*Frank*ly, everything seemed like it needed to be refurbished. This is the way Lucy wanted it because this is the way her grandparents wanted it, and that is the way it stayed.

When Jana saw them sitting there she *impulsive*ly shouted: "Papa Pali! Mama Mai!".

At that moment Jana behaved as if she were still that little girl from long ago.

An excitement and a familial stream-of-happiness *Glided* inside Jana's whole body.

This infantile behavior Jana had not felt or displayed in a *lange lange lange* while!!!

 Papa Pali and Mama Mai were also very excited at seeing Jana, their great-grand-daughter.

The old couple stood from their chairs and headed toward Jana…a feeling of connection *between-generations* seemed to pull them together as though they were one.

[and that is because they have always been {*bing*} one].

Jana tried to tell them to wait for her in their chairs, but the **EXCITEMENT** just overwhelmed any type of common-human communication.

Pure excitement and joy vibrated in that room!

A joy one finds *only when* loved-ones reunite after being separated *for-as-long* as **these-three** had been separated from each other.

The day of reuniting had come!

[Oh my! Beautiful J!]

…if only for a short while.

"w*hile*" in terms of *h*uman-*t*ime-*lapsing*.

All three embraced each other.

[what a beautiful sight indeed! J]

From a distance, it looked like a team huddled between plays: encouraging eachother for the next big play!

NEXT BIG PLAY!:)

They stood huddled for a long-*five*-minutes: taking in eachother's energy and greeting it with a unity of *one*.

While they were huddled, Jana felt the baby move within her…it was as though the little child within her knew *W*hat-*W*as-*b*eing-*t*ransmitted.

t w e l v e

The separation was a slow one as they all sat down near the kitchen where her great-grandparents had been waiting.

Jana talked about her new love in California, and her new child coming-into-the-world.

Jana only shared the things that brought her happiness.

Jana didn't want to burden them with her past problems in relationships and her insomnia and faint spells that came to her regularly (but not as frequent as in the past).

The *two* old *V*eteran's-*O*f-*t*he-*W*orld listened intently and nodded and grunted in intervals:

...indicating that they understood.

Numerological Wehrmacht

E I G H T

スケジュールされた殲滅
Sukejūru sa reta senmetsu

組織解体
Soshiki kaitai

While *the three* communicated, Lucy was in the kitchen finishing up the preparation for dinner.

When Lucy finished cooking she put everything down and turned off the stove and joined the group.

The moment arrived for Jana to inquire about her father.

Lucy was happy to be there with *the three* as she knew that this part in the conversation is very important for Jana.

"I want to know", Jana hesitated...

"What happened to Papa!!? "

"I want to know", Jana did Not hesitate...

'Where is Papa!!!?"

"where is papa!!?"...Jana yelled in anguish with streams of tears pouring from her face.

The couple just stood there not really knowing what had happened to their grandson.

They did not speak for they did not know. They just looked down in sadness as Jana's face continued to be filled with streams of tears that fell on her chest and womb.

C H E S T and

WOMB

There was a

s i l e n c e.

And then

there was another

silence.

And then

it was followed by another

silence.

**Schweigen   Schweigen
Schweigen**

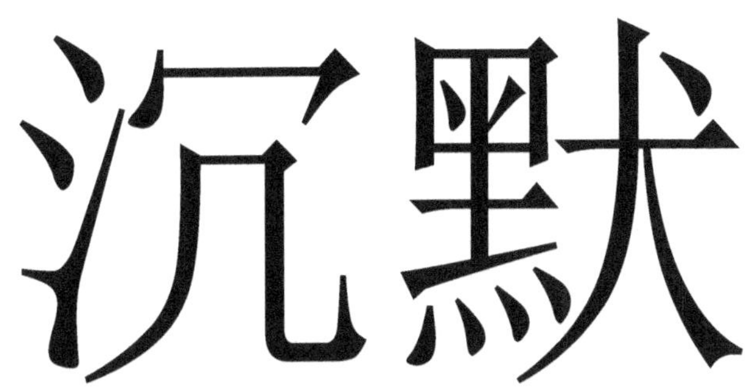

Lucy quietly stood and embraced Jana as she wept.

Suddenly **Mama-Mai** raised her head up high and stretched her arm toward Jana and placed her right hand on Jana's *left* shoulder.

Jana slowly looked up and "se fijo" into the **deep** eyes of her great grandmother.

The stare was penetrating:

s　　t　a　　r　　e

penetrating
penetrating

s   t   a   r   e

Jana saw something in her great grandmother's eyes she had never before seen.

seen before before seen

There was darkness in her pupils that began to transmit *a message*.

It appeared as though a white light was growing within-**M**ama-**M**ai's-pupil.

This growing light within the darkness of the pupil was *emitting* outward:

The *white- light* traveled to Jana and
EMBRACED

embraced her.

Mama-Mai began to speak an old Comanche dialect saying:

"My child: we are all one and to one we shall return."

"Do not feel sorrow for your father: wherever he is he will be with you forever."

Jana understood what **Mama Mai** said for she had picked up the language via a *translator*-within-the-*white-light*.

The **VERBATIM** Were Placed in Written-Words that Jana could see and understand!

Jana believed **Mama Mai**.

The energy that `held` Jana gave her **that** CONFIDENCE to *believe*.

Then

Mama **M**ai stood and *continued.*

Mama **M**ai lifted her arms to the skies and spoke:

"Long Long ago before the white man completely took over our lands (as was destined) my grandmother Shesha was designated to look over the spirits of the Earth."

"She is what-unites and maintains all beings to the one source of all..a source we are all part of: ...the Giver."

Jana began to tremble in fear: for *that name* was the name she was given in her recurring dreams.

Jana kept silent but began to feel faint.

Jana's pupils began to dilate.

As Jana began to go into another of her sudden loss-of-consciousness, she was awakened by the *waving* motion generated by her great grandmothers' hands.

Jana was brought back to *the first-consciousness* by Mama-Mai's **growing** ENERGY.

Jana began to see *elliptical waves* of white-light FILL THE ROOM as **Mama Mai** motioned *them* with her arms and hands.

"Shesha is in all of us and now that she has left the physical constraints of this world: she is very much alive in us all!"

in us all!

"She is still guarding the world and she beckons YOU-JANA to take your place in this task of one day joining her by becoming a growing part of her... to STRENGTHEN-THE-GRIP-AWAY from *the false gods* who seek to keep us in the physical: limiting who-we-really-are *before* the capture capture capture ...who-we-really-are."

"...part of the *light*..."

"...**before** ... the Creation...

...**before** the **R**ebellion!"

Lucy was dumbfounded for she had never heard her grandmother speak this way.

Lucy had forgotten the ways of the past (what little she knew).

Because of Lucy's disbelief in her past and the belief that only the white-man's-way-of-life was the true way: Lucy did not understand where in heavens her grandmother was coming from.

Papa Pali, though, just looked at his wife with such **profound** *respect* for what his wife was giving Jana to know:

...a knowledge **Mai** acquired **not** from a passing on from one generation to the next: for that had been *severed* in the boarding schools.

Rather, the *transmission-Of-information* was done via a ***supernatural-way*** **M**ama-**M**ai had been practicing *before* she left to the boarding school as a child.

It was a transmission **no ruler-of-the-world** could *extinguish* for it was **not bound** to this earth this world this realm this **5***th* Dimension.

For the first time in Jana's life, the story had now been passed to her.

Jana is now the one who is to strengthen *the thread* protecting energies from the Enemy. Energies captured and placed into encasements by the stubborn grip-of-determination of **Ra**!

Ra...a stubborn energy also known as *L*ucifer or Satan or [falsely] The *L*ight and many other religious names! names! names!

see see see!

Jana sat there invisibly communicating with her great grandmother and **the FORCE**.

Jana did not question her great grandmother. Jana instead nodded and grunted: indicating that she understood.

The *invincible* invisible communication emitting from the light surrounding the living room was all Jana needed to finally understand why-she-was-the-way-she-was (and had been for so so long: since before birth, before **conception!**).

As quickly as the light had arrived, the light left.

Great grandmother sat back down.

Lucy did not understand what had just happened and simply decided to forget about it (as most humans do to this day: forget about it; not look deeper into things; not questioning: simply take in the **propaganda**; the **manipulations** around them).:(

Lucy spoke, "I'll get the dishes out". She stood and went to the kitchen.

The smiles returned to the Veterans' faces and **a-conversation-of-memories** *erupted* where Jana shared her childhood adventures at the reservation during the visits she made when she was a little girl.

It was a beautiful moment.

Jana felt se*cure*.

Jana felt **complete** (although her physical emotions still longed for her father: she felt a peace within).

Jana's cousins and their families joined them for a beautiful and fun dinner.

After dinner, Lucy invited Jana for a walk beneath the light of the moon.

There was only one path: the road that brought her to the house…where all the surroundings were **s**tretches-**o**f-**b**eautiful-**d**essert.

Medieval *IJssel* in Deventer

attracting James Leslie's Bloody *Dragon*

Both women said good night to **M**ama **M**ai and **P**apa **P**ali: who were departing to rest in their room.

Lucy and Jana held hands as they stepped into the dirt road.

t w o   w o m e n   h a n d   i n   h a n d

Both women had smiles on their faces.

"My dear, I know how distraught you are about your father… my cousin."

"I too feel a lost not knowing where he is and if he is doing well or not."

Jana was going to interrupt but she hesitated.

Jana

h e s i t a t e d.

For although Jana now knew more about herself and a path away *from-this-existence*: Jana nevertheless still held the human condition of wanting to know with **a-tingled-feeling-of-longing**...which **lingers on** in a mind conditioned by the human encasement.

A mind that seeks to find refuge in satisfying that *fallacious* need.

…and that need for Jana was carrying **a sadness** brought about by her great longing for her father.

"I can tell you" Lucy continued "that he was last known to be near San Francisco, California."

 "He was staying with a friend there: another native with the name of Regene Mentrata."

"Wild Feather had told me this name on a phone conversation I had with him. Your father was very quiet about what he was doing in California. But, I insisted that he give me one contact name where he could be reached."

"This was over **20** years ago. I had made numerous inquiries because I had not heard from him."

"I became worried."

"I was given a San Jose address of this person. I mailed several letters to both my cousin and Mentrata...but there were no responses to my letters."

"I made an attempt to locate him. I took a bus to California. When I got there, to the address, there was no one there by the name of Regene Mentrata or Wild Feather."

"The one who answered the door said no such people resided there. It was a young couple who had purchased the house at 512 ½ North 4th St in San Jose, California."

"I was very uneasy and so I went to the local authorities in San Jose. No one knew of that name or my cousin's name."

"I kept at the search throughout the area and even went to San Francisco: I found no one."

Jana was at a lost.

Jana did not know her father had been in California.

"What did you do next?", Jana added.

Lucy continued.

"I went home. That was all I could do. So I was leaving my cousin to the spirits…trusting that wherever he may be… he has found that eternal happiness of being a child of the Earth."

After that confession, the walk continued **in silence**.

As they walked, Jana decided to begin her mantra of looking up into the sky and breathing.

Jana needed to be well for her baby inside her…she needed to be calm.

But most importantly: Jana needed to know that everything on this planet has a purpose, and that at the end: all will be made right.

All MADE RIGHT

...for the deceiver and its clans will come to an end: and all the energies of the Creation will go home.

…traveling wholly or in their elements: depending if they had or had not repented of their mutinous insurrections.

An insurrection that has caused much harm, much discomfort, much pain, much sorrow, much uneasiness to all energies involved whether at a conscious or unconscious manifestation.

The next day, Lucy woke up early knowing that Jana was due out by noon to catch her flight back to Los Angeles.

Lucy made traditional American pancakes, sausages, bacon, and 'over and easy' eggs. As Jana sat on the table, her hunger surged again!

again!   again!.   again!.

It seemed her baby needed all the protein to *grow-to-maturity* and *enter* the world healthy!

It was *6* a.m. and Jana's great grandparents also sat at the table with those beautiful smiles of theirs.

Jana got up and gave a big hug of love to her ancestral lineage.

Curiously, her great grandparents would not eat such foods presented to Jana: for they had kept the ways of old and preferred a light morning meal.

In the past free-nomadic-way-of-life (of which the Comanche were a part of and participated in): the old Comanche couple ate a similar (pre-Colombian) yet modified morning menu of:

Nuts and berries buried in a light corn cereal bread dipped in goat's milk.

In the past though, PEMMICAN was used instead of corn cereal bread!

The use of Pemmican was especially true when LONG travel was on the horizon entailing hunting preparations and surveyances, attached to an unpredictable availability of nourishments along the way.

Pali remembers as a very young child how this travel-food of pemmican delighted him: The flavor of buffalo meat grounded and mixed with berries and nuts and covered in melted buffalo

fat...yum yum **yummy:)!**

It was especially tasteful to **Pali** in times when the catch of new game took days to achieve.

A *p*ower-*P*unch meal all in one!

[oh my J!:)]

Mai remembers when Mama *Atstaka* would make soup using Pemmican. It would always be done near a river or lake.

a　s　t　a　t　o　s

八十五

nie odpowiedź

And although they had eaten a heavy dinner in their younger years: they knew better to have a lighter-late-afternoon-meal at their progressed years.

Lucy usually prepared 4 p.m. dinner for them that she knew they enjoyed: beans, bread, and a couple of slices of buffalo meat, or whatever there was available for Lucy to provide.

And now in the morning they became sort of Morning-Vegetarians...easing their intestines with vegetarian nuts and berry corn meal bread:)

These **Ancients** were not-picky-but-grateful.

CURIOUSLY, every meal Lucy provided the *Bloodline* was satisfactory and pleasant.

*M*ai and *P*ali

a ***revered*** gem-in-perseverance-and-love....

perseverance-and-love

An unbreakable bond-in-purpose....A non-*ending*-flare-of-Hope-and-Faith!.

a lineage to...

JĀNA

始發站

北角　　　　　　　　　西南角

角落東　　　　　　　　　南角

PART 6 of 7
SEARCHING FOR WILD FEATHER

Chapter Thirty
*W*ild *F*eather In *C*alifornia

Jana's flight home was bittersweet for deep down inside she longed to have *all-worlds*: a new life with Miguel.....her mother...and her family on the reservation.

The *renovation-of-contact* nevertheless was a starting point for a probable future.

Maybe, Jana thought, things will work themselves out.

Jana formulated **HOPE** f~rom WITHIN.

Jana formulated **FAITH** f~rom WITHIN.

Jana began trusting in *what-lies-ahead.*

V o r o v h e t e v

 Ultimately, Jana concluded: "I will be where-I-need-to-be".

At this moment though, all things pointed for Jana to stay in California.

Jana wanted so desperately to have that heterosexual-family she dreamt-of-with-Miguel.

Jana too wanted to complete her book.

على الرغم من هذه الأولويات ela alrghm min hadhih al'awlawiat, Jana's most pressing Esperanza on her list was to search for her father.

Jana knew her destiny as Shesha…despite *dat*, Jana wanted to gravitate toward her human form and its needs.

… and thus Jana wanted to search for her father.

A conflict between the doubts and wants of her human state and the certainty of her eternity existed for Jana: a *C*ontainment-*i*ssue that Jana and all humans struggle with till-their-last-days-of-*O*xygenated-*B*reaths!

That is, Jana did not fully grasp the supernatural world that she had experienced or that which awaits her *down*-the-line! …and so creating a conflict where Jana wanted and desired to be NormaL.

Jana wanted a NormaL life

to behave as NormaL as possible.

l'impronta della nostra esistenza Tweedles nella nostra mente!

And simultaneously the other parts of Jana wanted to explore her eternity.

CONFLICTS

Ultimately, though, Jana chose to be normal (as defined by a Western society) for as long as she could.

A *Struggle* Pulling the subject Away From *The Truth*.

How can these conflicts be resolved HERE?

They cannot.

It requires a certain 'carbon being' to have complete control over its containment to accomplish that in its entirety (and that is IF *the truth* being held is actually *The Truth*!)

There exist **few** who can accomplish **complete control** and **continual-thereof** over the containment. [Jesus Christ being the only complete conqueror of the containment!]

[Many fail in the struggle in the beginning: including the author of this book!]

As for Jana at that very moment in her life, she was leaning more and more unconsciously in blocking all supernatural occurrences which took prominence during her sleeping hours when she dreamt.

And so a struggle persisted within Jana as with every human and other carbons, because the deceit is so strong and well-crafted: so much so that it will-not-end here in this 5th dimension... because evil cross-roads have been created to carry forth an ultimate control by the enemy. [but the enemy will permanently fail ultimately. God Father is Greater in every way imaginable!] [Quark to

Elephant! No adequate comparison. Enemy has failed]

In-this-world **CaPtuRed** energies are at a constant **bombardment** as the **Fish-Đàng** realm stronghold is here...a servant of **Ra atua me** ē*tahi atu hunga tutu*.

A **Deceit** that seeks to conceal the truth which is:

we are eternal

No beginning No End

The Deceit implanted and fed to the human condition and other carbons.

The Deceit which seeks to destroy the unity of *The Oneness*.

The Oneness t[God Father] that brings everlasting joy, blissful, and nurturing existence.

The warmth of *The Love* that is lacking in quantity on this planet!

Miguel was waiting for Jana at the airport as she exited the security gates.

He had a bouquet in his left hand: six white roses and a *single-red-rose* in the middle.

Miguel was dressed in his usual business attire and looked so handsome…"Wow!", she thought, "I am getting out of shape and look at him!".

Jana so desperately wanted to talk to Miguel while she was in Oklahoma: but she resisted the temptation *knowing she* **nee**ded-**ru**flection-**ti**me.

Estonia

See on sama kõikjal ...
märkimisväärne kontroll iga piksli.

Miguel knew that and respected it: even though he was also tempted to call her or at least text her!

On Jana's ride back to Los Angeles, she reflected on the fact that in Oklahoma she had not written a single sentence for her novel...***Ona...Ona...Ona*** was too preoccupied.

Extinction piksli Gobblers on lõppemas

The laptop just came for the ride... unused.

At the airport, the greeting between the two was made with a single *kiss*:

No words where necessary to convey the longing that both felt for one another while apart.

The kiss seemed to last *forever*.

Both would not part lips and kept the warmth each felt of the other's lips close to their hearts...transmitting and penetrating through layers of membranes...sending a *signal-straight- to*-their-eternal minds.

The embrace that started softly slowly intensified.

It was a p***erf***ect COMPLEMENT to the kiss:

Taylor Series

Un continuo en todos los segmentos. ¡El Hilo irrompible!

It warmed them in the coldness of the baggage terminal and transported them (for a moment) to another place...all else faded in the background as they continued to **embrace** eachother.

J a n a w a s **h o m e!**

h o m e!!

h o m e ! ! !

Oh how wonderful it felt to be with Miguel again.

Oh how wonderful it felt that it was **a true presence** and *not-a-dream.*

Oh how wonderful it felt knowing that it was **not a faraway moment** WAITING to be *materialize.*

.....or **a want** or **an urge** or a use of **integration techniques** for something to eventually be found.

It was a *now*!

now:)!

Que bello.

As **the wanting** transformed **from the feel** to **the sight**:

Their lips separated and they looked at each other:

Their eyes MAGNIFIED with such an **intensity of love**.......that one cannot describe fully in words.

CANNOT DESCRIBE FULLY IN WORDS

words fully not

These Entities had found each other!!!!!!!

Or, had destiny united them?

In Jana's eyes, Miguel saw the **glimmer-of-light** which was **their-child**-*inside*-of-her.

Miguel did not know the sex.

Irrespective (at the end) it is **not the sex** which determines the **true-nature** of the being now within Jana.

Miguel was *just SO SO SO* happy to have a family.

All Three eagerly awaited a rich COMMUNION that (although limiting by the process of containment) translated **nevertheless** to a significant union for *an eternal* re-bonding!

At-that-very-moment: *all three* Smiled in Contemplation.

Smiled in Contemplation

At that INSTANCE: *all three* felt a common-UNBREAKABLE-thread.

Miguel's eyes represented HOPE and FAITH.

HOPE and FAITH [the Merris☺]

(And for Jana) a true BIRTH-FROM-FAITH to HOPE was to have finally met **the man** who truly loved her. [The Merrikis☺]

And, to have a child that represented that mutual love was beautiful!

Miguel

A man who willingly sought to care for her in *more ways* than she had thought possible.

Miguel   Miguel   Miguel   Miguel

Miguel!!

Jana recited his name as she Looked-Into-His-Eyes.

Hope
with Faith had
arrived!!!!!!!:)

The days passed beautifully.

The approximate days of about 4 groups of 25 passed beautifully!

Miguel and Jana both showed each other *more and more* love at a **Deeper level**.

 Romance was in the air

each-and-every-day
! ! ! ! ! ! !

Enseñanza

...and each and every night!**:)** [Oh my J!:)]

They would embrace each other after making love

.....they had learned to make love beautifully even with her womb so far *stretched* along.

rebenenud tagasi elementaarse osad...

need ei dismembered...

kaotamas nende identiteeti nende mässu

Despite the many wonderful moments, Jana was not completely at peace.

Jana constantly had her father in her mind and wanted desperately, more-and-more-each-day-that-passed, to locate him.

Initially Jana had looked for him through the Online *White* Pages.

He was not listed.

Then Jana began to type her father's friend's name:

She could not recall it.

What was his name?

It was?

It was?

was?

She phoned Lucy who gave Jana his name and last known address.

It was:

Regene Mentrata
512 ½ North 4th St
San Jose, California, 95112

Toward the end of her telephone conversation, Lucy counseled Jana not to have any expectations if she was ADA**Man**tly determined on looking for her father.

"Leave the events in the hands of **GOD**. Everything serves a purpose."

Jana thought about what Lucy said:

"**HANDS**-of-God".

"Who is God in this world?..." Jana thought.

"...but an **ABSENTEE** hidden entity!" Jana concluded.

"...an Obscure Being, A Fleeting Idea, A Powerful Metaphor of Us Not Here!"

of **US** Not Here

She contemplated some more:

"There is a definitive author or authors of this Creation but is it really **GOD**?" "Really?"

"Everything d**O**wn-to-the-last *element* known and unknown follows a ***designed*** pattern."

a ***designed*** pattern.

"Influences of one element on another is CONTINUOUS...making a DESIREd *end-result!*"

Jana continued:

"The exact quantities of all things set in motion have been measured out to an *exact* precision. Such precision that there is no known *public*-human-measurement-tool that can...can measure it!"

"Why is this god or gods hidden?"

Jana **BEGAN** to be directed toward a **REALIZATION**:

"they are hidden because.. the ultimate goal does not...

does not...

does not

benefit-us [we/u/i/them... over there look!!!]"

"We are pawns blinded to the extent that we have been trained to *blind-ourselves* and each other without even knowing it!"

Jana began to get **angr**y.

"Breathe Jana!", she told herself as she tried to calm herself down.

"**Negative Emotions** serve-no-good-**purpose** but that of keeping us from the truth!"

"And the truth is: we are slaves in this world. We are products!"

products!

PRODUCTS!
products!

Jana continued to breathe and returned to a stable medium in-her-mind.

Right-then-and-there Jana decided not to use emotions whenever she contemplated such *things*...

...*things* that most people do not even fathom!

Jana stood from where she sat and outstretched her hands at 52 degree angels from her trunk!

She SENSED-her-***condition*** and said:

"even these bodies we occupy are designed by these hidden false gods; these manipulators, these deceivers, these enemies!"

"They are not the True God…the Joy, the Peace, the Love, the Hope, the Faith…the One God who is trying to save us from these encasements before the rebellion is destroyed."

"Every-created-part has its *signature* of its maker from the number of digits our bodies have to the number of cells and chromosomes and all

the proteins that make up genes that give the
commands!"

And these encasements created not by the One
God are prisons, death sentences that are false,
manipulators in order to create a product for
consumption."

Jana closed her eyes: "What defines God or god or
gods!?"

"We-are-**PART**-of-the-Thread and
not-a-*product!* "

"not **a product!"**

[.......she said this angrily in secret!]

"And the clarity of the i-*enemy* is what the
deceivers fuzz and hold on to..." She continued.

"fuzzing the nature of the enemy in
order to meet their purpose:"

"*CON*-TROL."

"All the so called god or gods are all part of **The Thread** they-seek-to-separate-from..."

"but **cannot**."

"**cannot!**"

"even though they convince themselves and others otherwise!"

Jana stopped contemplating and tried **very-hard**-to-control-the-emotions within her.

Emotions that kept nagging on her like a persistent pesty bored-**cat** nags at its master for attention!

...nags at its master for attention!

nags!   nags!   nags!

At that moment: Jana decided that she would look for her father regardless of the conclusion.

Jana (aware of her restricted mind.......) decided to use it!

...to understand what happened to "daddy".

...to try to reconcile with her father: in terms of a long-absence-of-unintended-communication.

of unintended-communication

unintended-communication

Jana needed to know of him: "Where is he!?"

For now Jana refused to look to the supernatural world for answers.

Jana reminded herself that she wanted to be normal and figure things out in the normal human way {despite her knowing that it was flawed...contaminated by the *encasement* and its supportive created **environments**!}.

The date was

Venus Day
the 7th of *Mars*
2 Thousand and 8.

About 4 months of deep thought roamed Jana's mind to date.

At the present THOUGH, Jana felt she needed to be a detective-of-sorts...to piece together clues to help her *locate* her father.

Jana made arrangements to drive to San Francisco to gather any possible leads, and then *backwards* to San Jose.

Jana did not want to fly.

Jana felt she needed to stay as close to the ground as possible; as if the **dirt** (with its energetic fields) was beckoning her to stay near.

Miguel was made aware of her decision that night.

Miguel knew that her father Wild Feather had been on her mind consistently.

...and that she was SEEKING-ANSWERS.

In Jana's pregnant condition, Miguel would not feel comfortable having her *go-alone* to investigate.

Miguel wanted to protect her.

Miguel loved Jana deeply.

And ALSO honestly…

… *YET* honestly...

honestly

… Jana did not seem *altogether* in-her-mind.

To Miguel, Jana looked distressed and anxious.

Miguel made-up-his-mind that he would travel with his *wife* on her search:

...and let the company run itself (with his top-tier management team at the helm).

Miguel's *wife* Jana is.....the closest thing he had-ever-had-to-another-human-being on an

amalgamated

emotional,

physical,

augmenting-spiritual level.

Jana protested saying that Miguel needed to take care of his businesses.

Jana did not want to be a burden to her husband.

Jana told him, "Everything will be fine on my own..."

"and that... that ...."

Miguel gently neared himself to Jana and whispered in her ear.

"Enough Jana"...(he said gently.)

Miguel continued *in-whisper* (inhaling and exhaling at her right ear).

"You are my purpose."

"You are **the-one-I-love.**"

Miguel paused and breathed a little more:

"It would be ridiculous for me..." He took a long breath, then said as he exhaled,

"...to let you go alone on your journey." another breath.

"...to find your father."

Miguel **slowly-and-gently** separated his head from Jana and looked Jana straight-into-her-eyes and said:

"You are *my-first-priority* Jana."

"And I love you."

Jana began to sob at those precious words...hearing them in her mind:

"my-first-priority...I love you."

Jana knew she could not convince Miguel otherwise.

Jana sobbed and sobbed and sobbed.

Miguel held her close to his heart.

Both stood there...embraced in each other's arms

Both very-much very-much...*in-love*.

At si*X-a*nte-*M*eridiem...

M**o**r-ning-before-*MOON*day, the 9th of Mars 2 Thousand and 8, Jana and Miguel parted Santa Monica California and took the 101 North bound route to

eclectic San Francisco.

The distance was just *under* 385 miles; driving at a n*orm*al pace: they would *arrive* in San Fran*cisco* at around 10:20 a.m.

C begann krumm und weiter bis zur Gegenwart. C ist ein Arm der Regierungen gehören, ... in Einklang zu steuern (und verteilen) zentralisierte Technologiewissen für die größere Amplitude der Kontrolle.

Miguel had insisted on making all of the accommodation bookings: they were to stay at the **downtown**- St. Regis Hotel.

Prior to their departure Miguel had sent an email to his Los Angeles *management* teams, asking them to make an announcement for him at the combined New Year's party at one of his com*pany*'s Los Angeles *headquarters*.

The message was simple:

"Due to a family *emerg*ency Miguel would not be able to attend the celebration tonight. He wishes everyone nonetheless much love and a wonderful New Year!"

The New Year was *celebrated in* **March** rather Than January... as that was the company's **Fiscal** *new year*!

Miguel made it a point EVERY-YEAR *dur*ing-this-time to give large monetary gifts to the most loyal of the staff: those that went beyond the *line* of duty to help his businesses grow.

Those that were not much inspirational the year prior to the celebration would receive a tangible-gift of much *lesser value.*

The yearly gift-method was quite the indicator for all of Miguel's personnel to gauge to see if they needed to improve to reach the large monetary gift level.

It also served as an unspoken-warning to those receiving just tangible gifts.

The indirect message was simple:

...they had better improve their commitment and attitude if they *cherished* working for a company that paid **well**-*above* the national norms (which included lucrative fringe *bene*fits that gave 4 weeks paid vacation to each employee per year instead of the standard 2!).

The fortunate thing, for everyone-involved-in-the-companies, is that 97 percent of all of the staff **received** large monetary-gifts, along with a surprise package that usually included *two* paid round *tr.i.p.* air fare tickets to a location of their choosing!.

[Oh my J! Where do I apply?!!!:)]

hävitatud

[**Istanbul** Here we Come!!!**:)**]

[please please **cevizli baklava!** **yummy Yummy!:) ...]**

[**with a tall glass of beer! eh yeha!**]

[**feed feed baklava too... with coffee in the morning!:)' ooh yeah J!:)**]

The morning was clear and beautiful, with a temperature of 43 degrees and decreasing as they neared the *North*.

...but gradually increasing as the sun took prominence over its existence!

Jana scrambled through her paper work as Miguel drove.

Miguel kept quiet because he knew Jana needed the time to plan out and investigate for any clues to her father's disappearance.

Jana had read about the Alca*traz* take over by Native Americans protesting the continual injustices the federal government had imposed on the original peoples of North America.

Jana also read the arguments to redress the hundreds of U.S. peace *treaties* **imposed-on** the Native Americans that were consistently broken by the U.S. Federal government: taking away Indian lands in all states (**imposing-migrations** on the Natives) and thereafter giving the stolen lands to the planned Anglo-expansion.

A FORCED MIGRATION

Imagine: someone comes knocking at your door with weapons pointed at you and your loved ones and tells you: "**Get out!** You are *no longer* permitted here. This is **our** home **now!**"

"**You**, yea **you!**"

"Move over there, several thousands of miles [and to another several hundreds of miles] and that is where you will go!"

"We set the boundaries of your *existence* now."

"And if we need **that space later**, we will move you **again!**"

"Got it!"

And the thousands of Native American tribes were moved again and again and again!

Many of these reservation lands were very inadequate for growing crops. And if they attempted to grow anything...many times they were relocated again in favor of giving those lands to the White Man.

The continual push from promised treaty lands to other undesired locations was *not ideal.*

...a constant-reassignment-of-forced-migration increased in the mid-to-late 1800s.

This was devastating to an already devastated-displaced-humiliated-spit-on-population (the first inhabitants of the Americas!).

Toward the end of the late *Twentieth* Century, the lingering remnants of the Native Americans argued for more self-*determination* on the present day reservations laid out in particular parts of the created Jewish state: the United States of America.

The surviving Native Americans also desired a take-back of some of the lands illegally taken, asking for at least those lands not used:

...The Discards!.

D i s c a r d s

The remaining N*ati*e Americans knew they would most likely never regain their original lands: so they at l*e*ast sought those la*nd*s not occupied.

And now into the more recent future, was the descendant of Wild Feather, the **remnant** called **Jana**.

Right before Jana's departure from Oklahoma, Lucy gave Jana a book that WILD FEATHER kept with him. He had accidentally left it behind when he departed to San Francisco THAT-LAST-TIME.

[Or was it an accident?]

The book discusses aspects of the plight of Native Americans caused by the newly-formed North American ***i*mperialist-Jewish-*g*overnment** known a*ss* the:

United States of America.

The author of the book is:

Vine-Victor-Deloria, Jr.

The name of the book:

"Custer Died for *Your* Sins: An Indian Manifesto".

Jana kept it with her as the *only-remaining-thing* her father had *touched* before he left.

On the now morning trip to San Francisco, Jana intermittently held it in her hand. Jana was *grasping-it-firmly* from time-to-time when she became impatient of *not having* found any definitive clues.

As Jana loosely clasped the book on one of those intermittent times by its front-cover (in order to place it back into her purse)

...a *small* *slip-of-paper* from within-the-pages (pages Jana had not seen before) began to fly!!!

This small slip of paper, that had flown from within a page of the book, was about to go through the driver *window* when Miguel saw it twirling around his face and reached for it.

[long sentence. Yea! J.]

"What's this?" he asked *grasping* the paper.

"I don't know" Jana replied as Miguel handed it to her.

As Jana neared her face to the-single- *small* - *slip*- *of-paper* , she saw names on it. The size of this paper was 7 centimeters by 16 centimeters.

On it was a list of names with phone *numbers*.

It read:

Regene Mentrata
(408) 742-2982

Bauistos Semrosa
(650) 889-0990

Malita Soches
(650) 889-0979

Jeremi Brian
 (415) 798-2537

"Four Names and *Numbers* written on it." Jana told Miguel.

"and one is that of 'Regene Mentrata': the guy my aunt Lucy told me my father was staying with up North."

Silence began as Jana tried to make sense of the list.

It definitely meant something:

...information that Wild Feather had in his book when he accidentally left the book behind.

These were contacts but of what sort: friends, work companions, relatives?

Jana pondered them as she typed each name on the Internet using her Notebook PC.

No one was listed.

...No one *except* Jeremi Brian.

...the-last-**one**-on-the-list!

In the search engines Jeremi was listed as a ci*vil* rights attorney (still in business and using the same telephone number!) [how antiquated!:)]

He had his current office at a downtown high rise on the 39th floor in San Francisco.

 The address was....is

606 Kali4Nia Street
Suite 3901
San Francisco, California
94111.

Jana called the office and requested an appointment with Mr. Brian.

Jana told the receptionist that it was about her father, "Wild Feather".

"Mr. Brian is in court at the moment. I will *relay* the message when he *returns* late this afternoon."

The rest of the drive was mostly quiet, non-disturbing, and beautiful.

Both **Love Birds** took in the open mountainous plains and glimpses of the Pacific Ocean.

At times though **restlessness crept up** on Jana (noticeable by her long-silences with dilated pupil stares).

Miguel let her be.

"There is a nice restaurant just off the 101 near San Jose, would you like us to stop for lunch?", Miguel suggested.

Jana broke her silence and nodded yes with a smile.

After about 7 miles, Miguel pulled off to a street named *Yasmin* and then a right to a parking lot with a building-decorated-with-American Colonial-Spanish-Carts.

[nice:)!]

The restaurant was called:

"Mexicanos Para Siempre".

As Jana *looked-up-at-the-sign* she smiled at Miguel, clasping his hand in enjoyment of the name.

They both *giggled:*):)

Jana knew Miguel was proud of his heritage and that made her happy.

Jana kissed Miguel's right hand and caressed it as he parked the car.

Jana's happiness **surged** *at-that-very-moment*.

For *that-instant*:

nothing existed but *them* in-that-place!!!

It was as though Jana had forgotten where she was going or where she came from.

[oh my J!:)]

Jana only knew that she loved the man next to her *so so so dearly*.

Jana was grateful to the *Four-W*inds for sending Miguel to her.

him to her

"Te amo",

She-Said softly to Miguel as he removed the key from the ignition.

"¡Te amo **más!**",

Miguel replied with a gentle kiss to Jana's lips.

Miguel caressed Jana's left cheek with his nose.

They both embraced each other (awkwardly in their seats!).

From a distance it appeared as though they were

manikins!

[Don't we all look awkward in these *bodies*!]

Both Jana and Miguel started being physically more careful with her growing pregnancy.

Regardless

Love took center-stage at that moment,

dissolving everything else from their minds

LOVE LOVE LOVE LOVE LOVE LOVE LOVE

Chapter Thirty One
San Francisco

The car landed at the Downtown San Francisco St. Regis Hotel at around 1:47 p.m.

The enormous buildings the downtown area had to offer seemed too big for Jana.

The downtown buildings gave Jana a sort of *phobia*...she felt enclosed in a *cage*.

Jana breathed and made the best of it; it was a temporary stay in the realm of earthly man-made MONUMENTAL structures *not an eternal one*:

...that conclusion consoled Jana to control her asthma-like-symptoms presently lingering in-her-mind!

Jana remembered downtown Los Angeles and how she avoided going there for the same reason.

Jana was used to rural Oklahoma with its open and breathable space existing up to her present time.

Fortunately, San Francisco offered many other areas besides this area of Monster Structures.

As Jana entered the lobby of the St. Regis, she felt lost.

Yet, it was beautiful to walk in and see *vases* with elaborate flowers decorating the lobby.

And the suite on the 34th (-7th) floor was gorgeous.

Jana had never been in such a suite before. It had a living room, bedroom, a kitchen, a sauna, a business suite office room, breath-taking views of the city, and much more!

As the bell person left the suite, both occupants of this temporary stay embraced each other.

For the first time in a while, both were together in an elevated structure grounded to a street!

"So I'll be on the phone for a short while Sweetheart." Miguel said.

"Try to relax and please be patient. Answers will come." Miguel assured Jana.

Jana nodded yes, kissed Miguel gently, and walked toward the large glass window to take in the city view.

Miguel walked into the suite's office room to make some phone calls to his *corpora*te managers.

Jana was hoping to get a call from Jeremi Brian *soon*: the only person who may or may not have a clue about her father's whereabouts.

Jana took deep breaths and tried to calm herself.

Jana was grateful that this Mr. Brian still existed: since the others appeared to have vanished!

v a n   i s h   e d!

From the time they had left the restaurant, Jana began calling the other numbers written on the small piece of *paper*.

Unfortunately the effort was a dead-end as those numbers had long been reassigned to other people.

Those that answered did not know any of the names she was asking for during her telephone conversations with these *new-recipients*: these *other-end* people of numbers dialed said they knew-no-one by the name of:

Bauistos Semrosa

or

Regene Mentrata

or

Malita Soches...

In Jana's mind, these individuals became

GHOSTS!

After a while Jana headed to the bedroom.

She sat at the edge of bed and began to meditate.

Jana knew she needed to calm down. It was not her *body-alone-anymore*.

"I must care for my unborn child within me", Jana said to herself in her mind.

Leaning back Jana lay her body down and closed her eyes.

She then began to chant:

"God Father Brings Hope and Faith For Those with no Hope and Faith"

"God Father Brings Hope and Faith For Those with no Hope and Faith"

"God Father Brings Hope and Faith For Those with no Hope and Faith"

"God Father..."

At the fourth repetition of "God Father" Jana fell asleep.

As the ***passages-of-time*** straightened-into-one

Jana transported.

Jana was no longer in the room but in the plains...again smelling the ground for buffalo.

Shesha spoke:

"Father, they are moving to the 2nd wind, going against the wind."

Father raised his hand and pointed to the direction indicated by Shesha.

The warriors *roar*ed their horses in the direction of life*!*

Life for the Comanche was the buffalo.

As they increased their speed toward the buffalo, they began to chant, praising the-*cycle*-that-sustained-them.

The *G*reat *B*eings moved toward a water *hole*.

After momentarily pausing in meditation while taking in all of the world's variables, Shesha jumped onto her horse and began to quickly follow the Buffalo's scent.

....little by little Shesha began passing the other warriors with such speed that when they turned to look at her,

…they only saw

the hoofs of the hind legs of the gift from the Europeans.

(In reality a gift on a planned course!).

Approaching within 25 strides of the buffalo-herd Shesha *peered* into *the* right *eye* of the b*ulk*iest buffalo.

Shesha rode on the right side of *the Beast*!

IN ITS EYE *Shesha saw* a light that began to **G R O W** in size UNTIL all around her became *white!*

Shesha was *in spirit* once more...waving her entity from left **to** right **to** up **to** down.

Energy flowed from this spirit-entity: having a controlled-energy Shesha did not understand completely; nor did she care to do so.

At that moment, Shesha again began to understand her purpose.

Her energy of power glided with penetration through all the grounds of the Earths and beneath to the core of the Earth and to the ends of the other side of distant stars and Beyon!!!

Shesha became a web-of-energy that *weaved-out* the spirits-of-doom ripping them from the Earth and Other Energy Powers (OEPs) and back into **The Thread** in a refinement process where they were captured and held at a station.

The Processing Station.

...ever refining

…ever purifying

...ever preparing

for the return back Home from which they came.

A reminder to the wise: prior to the Contamination, by energies whose separation from the **Unity** began with **a thought**

 in a Designated Place

and then they expanded away from ***The Thread*** and into the **Rebellion**, peace and love existed amongst all energies IN God Father.

Where did these **spirits of doom** originate *from*?

What where their origination space?

Where did the contamination process envelope them into obedient programmable **malicious beings**?

from Earth?

from Sun?

from Thought.

.......Shesha knew not.

Shesha only knew her being was an energy that sifted the Earth and Distant Planets and Stars preparing the dismantling of all programmable **malicious beings**, and preparing the liberation of imprisoned and deceived energies from strong and stubborn contaminants known as the Rebels.

...**malicious beings,** created energies programmed to contain and convert the prisoned energies for consumption.

Energies like Shesha were assigned to minimize the **spirits-of-doom**'s reach.

9 Universes sought the consumption, vying and fighting for the resources...The Rebel 𝕮reation is plural not singular!

The Thread is singular...the *True and Only𝖚niverse.*

To preserve the harmony within the True and Only Universe, the 9 rebels, the rebellion, were expelled from the Universe, like one that spits out poison from one's mouth.

Shesha knew not the *mysteries* hidden.

....for Shesha was not assigned the end-result but rather a `Maintenance` to keep the expansion of the 𝕽ebillion in check.

Shesha was part of the (so called) **B**lack **H**oles quietly bringing the **9 𝕌**niverses **9 𝕽**ebellions **9 𝕮**reations to a preparation for CLOSURE.

Shesha was and is an

INSTRUMENT-OF-FILTRATION!

Shesha had no desire *to know* but to let loose the energies from her being. Shesha knew her limitations for it had been programmed into her.

programmed into her!

She had *a limit*!

$$\lim_{n \to c} f(n) = L$$

a measure.

At that moment, after oscillating to this limit, the light became dim.

…and then dimmer

causing Shesha to return to her body that was riding on The Horse.

As Shesha entered-her-limitation, she pulled out her bow and with a single arrow released it toward *the old beast* belonging to a pack of *seven* buffalo.

The arrow flew straight into *the eye* where she had entered the *white-light*.

The beast was caught by surprised at the accuracy of *that*-woman-on-the-horse and fell to the ground.

The beast stifled and sought to shake off the arrow which pierced its eye and went through its *brain*.

....blood gushed out of the beast and it began to lose its source of bodily life.

The other warriors quickly released their spears at the beast: aiming them at its he*art*.

...putting the beast into *the next* life!

The remaining six buffalo continued their journey to Unknown Territory!

the *Seventh* lay dead.

....providing nourishment for the tribe.

In that tribe Shesha *reigned* as the greatest marks shooter ever known. Her legend transcended to other tribes in the region as well.

Neither her father nor the other warriors knew of the light which Shesha had transformed into (for they-do-not-seek-separation).

[as most humans do not do today as well...unawares-of-the-danger-underlining-their-existence-in-this-realm.]

[*Una*wares that ignorance as to their true-self puts them in Magladized-danger...easily lied to and manipulated for a detriment end-result OBLIVIOUS to the subject]

[And to the subject (*you*) I say:]

[A w a ken!]

Shesha knew best to keep it a mystery.

Back in the tribal community the people smiled with contentment as the warriors brought food and skin for the living.

It was a wonderful catch and a feast that night was made in honor of the Warriors of God who they are a part of...Warriors that provided them with nourishment in an uncertain world.

Each member of the tribe knew in an unconscious level that they formed part of the Eternal Energy away from the Earth world and the litter of scattered Stars [the 5th Dimension]. A formation before the Creation [the Rebellion].

And although a "conscious" consistency of the nature of God differed amongst the tribes of Comanche and other peoples: neither group took the arrogant stance of dictating a religion and violently and involuntarily imposing it onto the world!

These **Pushers** had motives beyond spiritual enlightenment: Control.

Why is that?

Why is what?!!!

Simple:

The world is also littered with *demons* (manipulators) and one cannot even fully trust oneself in this containment (human body or other carbon organism encasement) because it contains "manipulators" that distract oneself of the true nature of our *Origin*.

And so each tribe understood that higher level comprehension, hidden from each one of us, cannot be fully grasped or attained so long as one occupies this realm.

And the ideal of a "perfect nature" and a "perfect being" cannot be achieved here. [Except for the Jesus Christ, our Savior]

How can a prisoner fully achieve peace here?

How can a prisoner fully achieve perfection "perfect being" here being bombarded by these demons?

How can a prisoner fully achieve "perfect nature" while in chains?

It cannot. It cannot be achieved.

[Only Christ Jesus Achieved This…hence the only way out of here is through Him, The Chosen Lamb of God.]

Accordingly, for the Comanche other aspects of life took prominence (and so falling as the rest of the world does into confusion; into distraction).

As Shesha lay in her Tipi she began to hear water flowing from the sky.

Provoked Shesha got up and went to the door of the Tipi and looked up into the sky (no water was present).

Shesha slooowly swayed her head from left to right, and then Jana opened her eyes and was back in the St. Regis executive suite.

…water from the shower was running.

Miguel was in the shower.

Jana sat up slowly and took a deep breath.

...she inhaled with such control her surrounding, counting *segments-of-time* that materialized around her.

Slowly Jana *exhaled* t i m e ...releasing herself into *this present*.

Jana delicately undressed and stood naked in the warmth of the suite.

Jana unleashed the pink-band from her hair...letting loose her thread strands.

Jana then slowly began motions toward the shower of life.

Jana called out, "My love".

...walking into the shower with Miguel who gave her a passionate kiss.

They both cleansed each other *suavecito*: with such love and care...neither spoke but felt secure of having the other near.

Marzo New Year's Eve, both had decided to spend a quiet evening in the hotel suite in San Francisco.

The serenity alive that evening permeated the walls of the building.

...creating a peace.

... *the Serenity* sought to last the whole-night-long!

Its presence could not be denied or disturbed willingly.

It was being protected.

Shesha was in action that night beyond comprehension.

...to provide Jana-the-human the peace her encasement needed, in order to fully nurture the prisoner.

That peace was allowed an intrusion because of its planned development:

...the couple were *disturb*ed at 10:03 pm in the evening by a `single ring` to Jana's phone.

Jana reached for her purse. She had kept it near her because she needed that call.

Jana needed that call! that Hope! that Faith!

"Hello, yes this is her [7 second pause];"

"yes, perfect; thank you very much for calling [7 second pause];"

"yes, thank you and you have pleasant evening too [7 second pause]."

Jana placed the phone back in her purse and then smiled at Miguel.

"It was Jeremi Brian! He called!! Oh my God!!!"

"He said we can come to his office tomorrow morning at 10:00 am!"

Chapter Thirty Two
A Meeting With
Jeremi Brian, Es*quire*

Morning dawned like a new life *clutching time* by its heels **into the depths of the segmented.**

Shears of light penetrated the living…within their dream and into the spaces-**in**-time.

The Fungwo 蜂窝 was full!

Jana slept well that night.

They had turned in to their bodily-rest at *a minute-past-midnight* with a beautiful kiss filled with love.

A radiation of everlasting love of

un*breakable Hope and Faith*

un*breakable Hope and Faith*

un*breakable Hope and Faith*

energized their existence that morning!

The warmth of the bed sheets were **irresistible**!

They felt like **pearls of cotton** warming every crevice.

The occasion was like one-of-those-mornings where one can sleep **all day long***!!!!!!*

Mmmm.

literally!!!

...the beings enjoying the bed and forgetting the world!:) [uuu la la ¡a sí me gusta!:)]

Jana slept on and on and on.

...until the ring of her alarm *robbed* her from her sleep!

It was 8:30 a.m.

Miguel had woken up 3 hours before, doing errands on the phone in a crevice within the hotel.

That night Both beings in the bed had slept with *such peace* that it seemed like UNMARKED-TIMES shut down *the tickings and the tockings*!

Both felt rested and assured.

At 8:53 a.m. they headed to the restaurant down at the mezza*nine* floor.

Jana craved eggs, pancakes, syrup, milk, and hash browns.

Jana ate so much that it was noticeable that her pregnancy was on *full-throttle*: she did not hesitate to meet the needs of the being within her.

Miguel smiled and was happy that his love was eating like a HORSE!!!

At 9:34 a.m. they took a taxi to the building of Jeremi Brian…less than a mile away.

Jana sat quiet, thinking, feeling the emotion in her and wanting desperately to get the answers to be able to see her daddy again.

Jana missed him so.

Jana missed his smiles.

Jana missed his humorous *pranks*.

Jana missed his excitement for the outdoors.

Jana missed his hugs.

Jana missed his kisses.

 Jana missed his calling her "my Pumpkin". [Oh my J!:)]

Jana loved the walks she had with her father. She remembered being picked up from school and going on new adventures in the open plains!

OPEN PLAINS!!!

During those excursions, Wild Feather shared some stories about roommates he had before he met her mother.

Jana remembers hearing a story about Sal*anger* (a roommate Wild Feather had when he first left the reservation):

Salanger was walking to a local *Circle K* clutching an umbrella with both hands during a fierce rain.

As Salanger reached the corner of the sidewalk to cross to get to the store, a pick-up truck zoomed around and splashed mud all over his clothes!

...making the umbrella he was holding *useless* toward any protection.

SalAnger had to run back home, shower quickly, dress quickly, and head-out to work *without* getting his usual cupcake and milk at the Circle K:'([Oh my!!! ¡lo siento Salanger!]

Jana met this Salanger years later as *Wild Feather* had kept-in-touch with him; but Salanger was off to college where Wild Feather had no interest of going.

Rather, Wild Feather wanted to work and live! ...to take in what life had to offer!

As Jana and Miguel *rode-up to floor 39* of the building where Jeremi Brian worked: Jana began swelling up with emotions.

Tears began to roll-down her face.

 Miguel held her and comforted her: not saying a word but giving *more than* words can *ever* give in times-of-distress.

As they got off the elevator, Jana stopped and looked at Miguel (holding his hand tightly).

tightly!

[a gripping tension of years of unconscious anguishes...culminating to this moment in time.]

Jana was sobbing quietly.

"I...I...I..",

Jana began to say.

Miguel just held Jana as she was unable to speak.

As they stepped out of the elevator, they paused in place.

Taking deep-*deliberate*-breaths, Jana *slowly* composed herself (wiping away the **tears** with her left hand. She left the hand moist from the *outside*).   *left   left   left!*

Tears from the *inside* of her being, Jana was NOT able to wipe away

NOT able to wipe away

NOT able to wipe away

With her right hand, after *61* seconds of elapsed time, Jana took a deep breath and shook Miguel's hand and smiled at him:

"I'm ready *SweetHeart*".

Both *walk*ed to suite 3949. [9 is a place holder. This world's constant]

It was at the end of the HALL-WAY, just *left* of the elevators.

It was the last door to the *right*.

left right

As Miguel *open*ed the office door, they found a small tiny *reception* area with a single woman typing on a desk just behind a *low-barrier* that created the receptionist counter.

"I'll be with you in a moment." the woman said as she continued to type, wearing a Dictaphone headset.

She stopped and rose to greet them.

"Hi, my name is Martha. You must be Jana. You are here for the 10:00 a.m. appointment?"

Jana nodded yes.

"And your friend?".

"My fiancé", Jana said *quick*ly, feeling a sort of a *battle* for the man of her life!

"Oh", Martha said **rather** dis*appointed*.

"He's *taken*". Jana nodded with a smile.

"Please have a seat and I will let Mr. Brian know you are here."

Martha walked *off* behind a door *frame*.

16 feet from the corridor door frame, at the end of the corridor, the last door to the right, Martha gently knocked and then opened the door.

Martha **poked** her head inside, stood still for a while, and then closed *the door* in front of her.

Martha walked back to the reception barrier.

"Please *follow me*. Mr. Brian will *see* you now."

[*What follows* in one's mind **often** *seeks an outlet into the depths of despair.* Beware! ignore them. For the true companion of one's mind is only God, who is All Peace, All Joy, Always Bringing Contentment, and True Resolution. **Anthying else, in this world,** that ruffles uncomfortably in the mind, is an agent of the Enemy!!!]

A tall white man, around 6 feet 7 inches tall, with a large, strongly well-built frame, bald head but grey hairs still neatly behind the ears, and a face like a monument made of rock (showing all the grooves-of-time with permanent creases created by the sun and by the dying cells and by...) greeted them:

"Come in and please have *a seat*", the man said with a deep **basso profondo** voice. This man was located behind a large legal desk that was occupied by several stacks of legal case documents, neatly laid out on it.

Jeremi Brian was a white man with freckles all over his face and hands.

He was a Ginger...with remnants still showing.

He wore a suit (a baby blue colored suit like from the American 1970's:).

Although Jeremi stood behind the desk to greet them, Jana could not see his pants' bottoms: but she *imagined* he had bell-bottoms! [hee hee hee!:)]

Jana thought: "Has this man *forgotten* we have moved on in fashion!?":). [J:)]

"This is my fiancé Miguel."

Miguel shook Jeremi's hand, smiled, and then took a seat in one of two empty chairs in front of the desk…the right chair facing the desk.

Jana remained standing, still with deep thoughts streaming in her mind.

Thoughts streaming in her **mind**

Jana was beginning to drift. Jana felt as though she was moving from the building.

She felt as though she was leaving her body [3-pronouns in one sentence! Strange]. Jana felt *strange.*

That was not out of the ordinary Jana, that >*strange*< Jana had experienced most of her life.

$$S = -(n_{\mathrm{s}} - n_{\overline{\mathrm{s}}})$$

"I can see some features on your face as that of your father," Jeremi Brian said.

"My father...my father" Jana replied sort of lost!

Jana began to focus her mind again and brought herself to the present position of her body.

Jana then proceeded to **raise** her voice with such *loudness* that it took Jeremi by surprise.

Jana yelled:

"**Where** *is my father*!!!".

"Please **Where** is my father!!!"

"Have a seat Jana, please!", Jeremi said firmly. He paused and looked straight into-her-eyes.

"Please", he repeated firmly but softly.

Jana stood unable to move.

<u>U</u>nable <u>T</u>o <u>M</u>ove.

UTM

Jana began to feel her whole body begin to *freeze*.

Jana needed to calm herself. Jana needed to do this for her *child.*

Slowly Jana reached for Miguel's hand.

Miguel rose and led Jana to her *seat* next to his.

Once Jana was *seat*ed and somewhat composed, Jeremi Brian spoke:

"Now, I could have given you the news over-the-phone last night; but I had to do it in person".

Silence seemed to m u f f l e -out-all-sounds at-*that*-moment!

"What do you mean in person? What news?".

Jana began to feel d i z z y.

The room began to *rotate* around her eyes. The walls where moving. The big glass window behind Jeremi Brian began to move.

Jana's seat began to move.

Jana was building up **so much** *energy* that it was not being dispensed or dispersed properly.

Jana began to feel the surge from within her soul.

"What ne**wS**!!!" Jana yelled.

This time Miguel became surprised and frightened.

He had never seen **her** like this before. [2 union pronouns…eternally bound!]

Jana became VERY AGGREssive as if she knew what Jeremi Brian was about to tell her.

Jeremi Brian *straightened* up in his chair and looked into Jana's eyes:

"Your father is **dead**."

A sudden **rush** of adrenaline and despair reached Jana with such INTENSITY that she began to **shake**-in-her chair.

"**No!, No!, No!, No! NOOO!**" Jana yelled from the BOTTOM of her lungs.

The room started to turn faster and faster.

Jana could not hold on.

She could not hold *on!!!*

Jana began to see *black*.

Her Eyes Dilated and rose toward her head.

Jana began to fall to the *ground*.

Miguel quickly grabbed her arm and pulled her up.

No more response from Jana was visible.

"Call a doctor, call an ambulance!"

Jeremi Brian dialed *911*.

Miguel laid Jana on the *ground* gently.

Jana had gone unconscious.

Jana had gone into a *coma*.

Miguel checked her breathing...he only felt light snippets of air *pass* robotically.

Her *pulse* was *faint*.

Miguel began CPR.

"Breathe baby, breathe".

Miguel kept at it *until* the paramedics came *in*.

a
point
of
death

Chapter Thirty Three (6)
Into The Light!

Silence

J ā n a

Chapter Thirty Four (7)
Roaming!

Movement.

Movements.

Slowing...

Breathing...

silence

J ā n a

.

Chapter Thirty 5
Transition On The Horizon

It was three a.m. exactly when Jana consciously opened her eyes.

Miguel was asleep at her side in a *chair*.

Miguel held her hand as he slept.

Jana *began* to feel-it.

It was the fourth-day.

Jana had been asleep for three-days-*straight.*

She had been in a *coma*!

For her to have awaken was beyond miraculous.

Jana had numerous needles plucked into her.

Jana began to feel the pain in her arms and legs.

...needle marks were numerous all over her arms and legs, with purple *shadings* ranging from dark to light.

It looked as if Jana had **leopard**-skin.

[Her species was becoming *extirpated* by the demons of the world...following their master's request. No room for Outsiders to interfere!]

Jana woke to a quiet and cold hospital *room*.

She had a bad taste in her mouth.

...it felt **extremely** dry all the way **down** to her throat and to her stomach.

Jana stared at the white wall in front of her.

Jana couldn't remember a thing as she tried to recollect *why* she was in-this-room.

What was she doing *here*? **uuh!**

Where had she been? **aah!**

Jana felt weak.

Jana had n e v e r felt *so so so* weak!

Miguel opened his *eyes* as he felt pressure from Jana's hand.

"*Mi Amor*", Miguel said softly...

....with a sigh-of-relief *emanating* from his eyes.

Jana smiled.

Jana really didn't remember what had led her to this cold *room*.

Jana tried to muster up some saliva to speak: she could not.

Miguel pressed a button by her hospital bed and a nurse came in.

The nurse had a face of relief to see that Jana had wo*ken*.

"Oh my dear: how are you feeling?"

Jana tried to make speech but could not.

The female nurse, a short Filipino woman in her early fifties (with short straight hair) poured *water* for Jana and carefully placed it near her mouth.

...slowly tipping some water over to her. Most of it went in, with some pouring onto a napkin the nurse held near Jana's chin.

The nurse took a sponge nearby and soaked it with water and fed it to Jana to moisten the cavity of Jana's mouth.

"That's better. Just relax dear: let the body react to the *water*".

"*Wa t e r.*" Jana's mind syllabized the phonemes ouuut onto her brain and they stayed there!

"I'll page the doctor to come and make a thorough examination of you."

"You look fine... just a little tired."

"Rest dear. I'll be back soon to check on you."

The nurse smiled at Miguel and went *out*.

Jana began to feel her throat feeling less dry.

She made a noise as she attempted to form a word. Her voice was HOARSE.

"Relax", Miguel said, "Just relax".

Jana nodded and attempted to reflect.

Jana worked hard in her silence to remember why she was there.

Suddenly, after sixteen minutes, her memory *recover*ed and she knew why.

...Jana began to tense up.

Miguel noticed immediately and repeated his words:

"Relax baby...Breathe. Take deep breaths".

Jana obeyed.

Jana needed to be well.

Her womb was visible and that brought her more resolve to control her emotions.

Jana needed to do it for their baby.

Jeremi Brian had come by every night to pay her a visit...he was due to arrive a little after 7 p.m.

Jana did not know of his visits but she began thinking that she needed to talk to Jeremi; Jana needed to know.

Jana slowly screeched out: "I re mem ber waaheeey Iam hhee".

...her natural voice slowly began-coming to *clarity* after every lapsed-word.

"I know dah mmmy fatha is noh he' anymo'; I muuust accep tha eveh doughe I do no wan ooo..."

"Je'mi wou'na lie ouh me...eee knu maiee fa'er."

Jana tried hard to pronounce the words correctly despite her feeling dizzy and not all there physically.

Jana paused a minute and a second and then said slowly:

"Now, I must *know... why...* and how."

Miguel listened patiently.

"Jeremi has come to see you during the last three nights...he is due to arrive later this evening."

Jana continued to *breathe* and to calm herself.

When Jana felt a moment of deep-aggravation from within her: she breathed deeper.

"Escape this web!" Jana thought.

"Restore my *health!"* Jana demanded from within.

"Restore my *health."* Jana began this word-mantra in her mind...

"Restore my *health."*

That evening, after about 16 hours of lapsed time in the day, Jeremi Brian arrived and was pleased to discovery that Jana had waken. He made the evening visit to Jana brief, she needed to rest.

He feared that maybe she would lapse into hysteria again. He did not want that to happen again.

"Tomorrow is another day Jana, tomorrow we'll talk some more. For now, please rest Jana." Jeremi assured Jana as he said his goodbyes for the night.

Chapter 36 (9)
An Accep**Stance**

The next Morning at the hospital had gone well. Jana's recuperation multiplied exponentially at every moment that passed.

The doctor had come in at 9 a.m. and checked all the vital signs recorded since her waking. They were normal for a pregnant woman of her age and stature. These "normal" recordings were remarkable considering the unstable condition Jana was in the first 3.4 nights prior.

The doctor couldn't figure it out: "normal!".

Prior to waking her pulse had been slow and her blood pressure was

low
low

low.

The doctor wanted her to stay one more night to monitor her. Jana, however, insisted on leaving.

Upon seeing that there was absolutely no brain damage, no signs of fatigue, no confusion, and seeing no other signs of red-flag indicators, the doctor agreed to release Jana from the hospital by 9 p.m. that night.

Jana dreaded the hospital environment and sought to move from it.

The baby was fine. All the I.V. nutrient fluids given to Jana had helped.

Notwithstanding, it was evident that Jana was thinner than she was three days ago.

Jana began eating solid foods after the doctor gave the okay. Jana ate little by little.

Jana consumed bits of squared potatoes marinated in extra-virgin-olive-oil (It was lightly flavored with *salt*).

Jana began to crave Cream-Of-Wheat and was given a bowl of it.

The contents looked deprived.

(lacking m*ilk* and sufficient s*alt* to her liking.)

With Miguel's assistance, Jana added whole milk, pure unadulterated butter, and a tad of salt to it:)

"mmm:) Better:) Thank you!"

Jana slowly consumed it, savoring every spoonful!

Miguel was happy to see her eat.

After this Unusual feast of hospital food, the rest of the late-morning went relatively quiet.

Jana kept up her breathing exercises throughout the day.

Miguel was in and out making calls to his business executives on the progress of his enterprises.

Miguel said little to Jana in terms of a conversation.

Miguel did not want Jana to exert herself or somehow become emotionally unstable.

Miguel wanted Jana to *rest*.

M[4].

rest.   *rest.*

Miguel had booked the same hotel rooms for their return that night.

In fact, Miguel had kept the same rooms since they arrived to San Francisco.

Both patient and patient-significant-other took mini naps the entire afternoon...BOTH slowly recuperating to *a-better-life*.

At *7:33* p.m., Jeremi Brian knocked at the door.

"Can I come in?"

...he asked from behind the door.

Miguel opened the door and greeted him; Jana did likewise.

"I am glad to see you doing better Jana!"

"Thank you Jeremi...I am sorry for my outburst the time I was at your office ...I..."

Jeremi interrupted:

"You need Not apologize Sweet Heart. I would have responded similarly...and I am truly sorry to have been the one to give you such news."

Each individual in the room took three breaths and then Jana responded verbally:

"I want to know why and how", Jana said.

"Jana, I don't want to give you any information to put your health at risk."

"Why don't you wait to speak to me at a later date when you have given yourself time; and after the birth of your child?"

Again each individual in the room took three breaths and then Jana responded verbally:

"Jeremi... I don't want to wait any longer. Please tell me. I have given it much thought and I am working on accepting this terrible news. I want to know *why-and-how*."

Jeremi pulled a chair next to Jana and sat down.

Jana lay in the hospital bed naked (covered only by a hospital gown and a thin-blanket.

"I will tell you."

Jeremi Brian hesitated for a moment, closed his eyes momentarily, and then began.

"Your father was part-of-a-group that sought reparations to the Native Americans that lost their lands by the numerous treaties made and broken by the U.S. Federal Government, and that were carried out in a variety of ways by their installed 'State' and 'Local' created governments (serving the regional power elites of course...or preparing a planting of elites to run the local governments)."

"Your father, Jana, participated in many protest events in the late 60's and early 70's. Wild Feather was part of the group that first occupied Alcatraz here in San Francisco."

"At that time I had just completed law school at Berkeley and I had joined a local law firm here in San Francisco."

"I wanted to help the movement. I believed in the movement. Consequently I joined in the protests and wrote letters for the inner-group known amongst themselves as the *Group-Of-Redemption*."

"Outwardly though: they were part of the general Native Americans present. Their inner-name was hidden, for the most part, from the general population."

"There were hopeful-days for *change*."

"However: their hopes were *marred* by the federal government cracking down on the protestors. The Feds' intervention became violent in certain situations."

"These 'certain situations' however were the ones made publicly: the physical 'violence' toward the Native Americans continued in a planned continual sequence and rhythm secretly...targeting group members (and their family members, if needed for persuasion)."

"The government also sent out covert special agents to quash the leadership through a variety of techniques that included secretly sending in moles and agitators within the inner groups (as well as bringing in non-natives into the struggle to justify a breakup of the protest...labeling the group as incoherent and 'not pure blood'."

"The infiltration to destroy their rights was in full swing…calculated and adjusted to meet the end goal: permanently disbanding the righteous protests."

"Hence, it gave the federal government fabricated-justification to end the Native American demands for Alcatraz and other **unoccupied** lands owned by the U.S. Federal Government around the country."

[and around the whole of the Americas…Not only in the U.S. but also in other lands now occupied and ruled by foreigners: Canada, Alaska, Mexico, Central and South America. Puppet regimes set to comply with the Elite in the U.S. or face unwelcomed aggression: Salvador Allende as a point in focus.]

[Thousands of points in focus existed and exist where leaders are toppled in order to maintain control…of human and natural resources…including the topple attempts made first with Hugo Chávez and then now with Nicolás Maduro in Venezuela. Fabricated corruption charges planned and put into action by the planted Elite within Venezuela, who control the food-chain distributions, and other vital economic components…causing economic chaos to the Venezuelen population as a whole, and promoting and promulgating the blame at the Elite's adversaries including Maduro.]

[How is this possible? The Elite (referred to by some as the Zionist, the Jewish hegemony) control all major Media in the U.S. and in the Americas and all around the world. It is ironic how the U.S. painted the Nazi Media as controlled when they themselves controlled THAT Media and the U.S. media networks, including television, motion picture productions, news, radio, commentaries, as well as all Major medias. The control is well set to brainwash the population in order to justify and execute malicious control on the population, their natural resources, and their true leaders.].

[…Vicious schemes to maintain control, not taking into account the lives of children, the elderly, women, and men, or animal around the world. Such cruel and selfish practices have been done for thousands of years by the power Elite that rule the world… at the expense of human life and of animal life.]

[And who controls these malicious Elite? It is true what the Bible says, "the whole world is a prisoner of sin" (Galatians 3:22)]

[And, "...the whole world is under the control of the evil one."

(1 John 5:19)]

["The great dragon was hurled down--
that ancient serpent called the devil, or
Satan, who leads the whole world astray.
He was hurled to the earth, and his
angels with him."

(Revelations 12:9)]

[And Jesus himself was placed into a sin
circumstance but defeated sin and the evil one:
"...the devil took him to a very high mountain and showed
him all the kingdoms of the world and their splendor."]

["'All this I will give you,' he said, 'if you
will bow down and worship me.'"

["Jesus said to him, 'Away from me,
Satan! For it is written: "Worship the
Lord your God, and serve him only."'"]

(Matthew 4:8-10)]

[But Hope and Faith are secured because...]

["We know also that the Son of God has
come and has given us understanding,
so that we may know him who is true.
And we are in him who is true--even in
his Son Jesus Christ. He is the true God
and eternal life."

(1 John 5:20)]

Jeremi Brian continued:

"Your father was among a group that were picked up by the Feds and taken to undisclosed locations...it was like a scene from the mafia: they came in with automatic guns in hands and forced the ones they considered leaders into two unmarked, windowless, black vans."

"I sent a complaint to the authorities but they just ignored it as if they had complete immunity from the big wigs on the top."

Jana listened with a very serious face as Jeremi spoke. Miguel sat in the back-seat quiet.

"Your father was a brave man, because many times he was in danger of assassination: yet he continued to fight for what he believed was long overdue for his people (who have been physically marginalized to this day!)."

"Wild Feather knew the risks."

"Days after the abduction I went to see Regene Mentrata...a friend of your father."

Jana immediately knew the name from the list on the little piece of paper inside the book her father had left.

Jana kept quiet and listened.

"Regene Mentrata was a **spook** when I visited his home."

"He did not even answer the door. It was about 2 pm when I arrived. After calling out his name: he wouldn't open the door."

"I went into the home by way of the side window:...all the curtains where drawn and it was very dark inside."

" 'What has happed?' I demanded him to tell me...he was sitting on a chair in the middle of a dark living room."

"Happiness was void there!"

"I turned on the lights and he squinted heavily...he smelled like he had not showered or slept for days."

"Regene looked completely **lifeless**. But he was breathing **not** dead."

"He was **alive**."

"Again I demanded 'what the hell has gone on here? Where is Wild Feather?' "

"Where are the others?"

"Regene began to cry."

"I let a minute escape time."

'What's going on man?' "I repeated to him."

"Regene yelled:"

" 'They're dead!' "

" ' **Dead!** ' "

"Regene then said he could not tell me more for he was threated to be killed if anything went public."

"After pressing him for some information: Regene told me that it was the Feds... and that they had brought him and Wild Feather to his house where they shot Wild Feather."

" 'They shot him in front of me!' "

" 'in front **of me!***/*' Regene began to cry."

" 'And worst of all they forced me to bury his body. It's over...It's over!!!' "

" '...you must not get involved further Jeremi or you will be next! I'm serious!!!' "

"From that point on the movement did begin to die down: men in leadership disappeared and the movement lost its momentum."

"I did not want to get involved further because I did not want to be part of something that caused people to lose their lives...I went on with my life."

Jana was crying quietly as she heard the story.

"I want to give my respects to my father...I want to visit where he was buried...where is this Regene Mentrata?" Jana asked Jeremi.

"I brought Regene to work for me when I got word of what happened to the movement."

"He is one of my legal assistants. He is better now but would rather not talk to no one."

"I did mention your name to him yesterday and your relationship to his Freedom-Partner-of-Past:"

"... Regene broke down and cried when I told him you were Wild Feather's only child."

"I must speak to him." Jana said.

"I must bring closure to this part of my life...I must visit my father's burial place."

"Listen Jana, I will speak to Regene and tell him about your request."

"You got to understand Jana...I had dared not ask him anything further back then because he was truly a *broken-man*."

"It took me more than *ten years* to have Regene change his outlook-on-life....to open up to a better life away from his mental anguishes (His environmental and involuntarily-induced-mental-illness.)"

With that said Jeremi Brian stood and promised Jana that he would call her tomorrow morning with Mentrata's decision.

Jeremi insisted though that Jana must respect Mentrata's decision.

Jana said nothing.

Jana just stared at Jeremi as he left.

Later on that evening, at *9*, the doctor arrived, checked Jana's vitals, and *released* Jana from the hospital.

After taking a cab back to the *Hotel*: both Jana *and* Miguel decided to walk a short block away from the Hotel to breathe in the San Francisco air.

It was cold but a pleasant walk in the downtown San Francisco area.

Both held hands and felt grateful that life had given *them* a second chance to move on with their *destinies* (*together*).

Chapter Thirty Seven
A Falcon In The Air!

"Mentrat will meet with you Jana", Jeremi Brian notified Jana over the phone the following morning.

"He will come to your suite to talk to you at about 10:03 a.m., is that okay with you?"

"Yes, of course, thank you so much Jeremi for making the time to see me, and for putting up with my emotions."

"It was a pleasure meeting you Jana, and feel free to contact me if you ever want to pay us a visit again or just to talk...okay?"

"Yes, yes, yes! Thank you!"

v   e   s   t   i   g   e   s

Jana hung up the phone and looked at the time. It was 8:00 a.m.

"Mentrata would be here in **123** minutes!", Jana thought.

The Mathematician within!

The Computationist within!

"In *7,380* seconds!", she thought further.

Jana was computing *numbers* in her mind.

[*Numbers* assigned by a defined-system which seek conformity for-all-those-that-use-THEIR-*numbers*.]

[All those that use (display-adjustments)-in-creativity in order to conform to *a set* plan]

[(*a set* **agenda**)]

[: **Something** written right-before the creation-of-the-Universes. The **Rebellion**.]

[A *Master* plan]

[A *Servant* plan]

[A *Reinforced* plan {a-set-of-de*cept*ions}]

o   w   a   r   i

[spell it out!]

Miguel wanted to give Jana her space. He wanted to provide her with space to help her bring closure to the sad-news of her father.

Miguel decided it was best if Jana meet this Mentrata alone.

The time was 9:03 a.m.: Mentrata would be here in an hour...an hour!

Jana felt uneasy to meet one of the men who last saw her father alive. The man who **buried him**!

Miguel kissed Jana at *9:47* a.m. and stepped out to meet a potential business client he had met in the lobby.

Miguel was due to return at around *11:00* am.

Jana was left in the room *alone.*

alone.

> *alone.*

Jana felt...

alone.

8ball...the 911 ball...the 666 ball!

Jana began to pace the suite.

Pacing was heard as Jana walked swiftly from one side of the suite to the other.

waiting.

waiting!

Waiting*!*

Jana had *not* called upon her growing-connection to-a-world-hidden-*underneath*-and-above-and-all-around-this-one.

One of those worlds is the world of her great-great paternal grandmother.

And in her time of need in San Francisco, Jana abandoned this altogether...allowing herself instead to be overcome

overpowered by her grief emotions.

Jana allowed the demons to creep up on her.

These demons, the so called hormones, took control of her time and of her *peace*, driving her to the point of death!

r   e   g   r   e   s   s   i   o   n

[a common symptom of humans]

[a programmed symptom *on* humans!]

[programmed symptom *ON* humans!]

Honestly, Jana found it difficult to con*centrate* and to continue to have focus.

Jana was too *consumed in-this-world.*

Jana was *enthralled* in its deceptions...coming closer to believing in them, **than** in-the-truth.

Jana kept trying to resist. But, at the end her emotions got the best of her.

Jana kept getting *clouded.*

c l o u d e d ! ! !

The moment had finally arrived:

Something *rang* from within her suite.

It was the suite's telephone.

The *RING* **seemed** delayed-in-time. It was as though it would *ring*-forever!

ring-f o r e v e r !

The pitch **seemed** strong with lots of reverberation coming from the **air***!*

Jana turned to face the phone and stopped her pacing.

Jana looked at her watch. It was *9:56* a.m.

Was he early?

What was the purpose of the ring!?

Purpose!?

Ring

Ring

Purpose!

Jana picked up the phone.

A voice said:

"*Hell*O, this is the reception desk...there is a Mr. Mentrata here to meet you."

"Should I send him up?"

"Yes! Please send him up.", Jana responded rather desperate and withOut a "thank you!".

withOut a "thank you!".

SIN a "thank you!".

Within *7* minutes there was a knOck at the door.

The time was exactly

10:03 a.m.!

Jana opened the door and *there...there* *There.* stood Mentrata.

Mentrata was a tall man of about *six* feet *four* with long gray hair and dark skin.

Mentrata was dressed in *black* slacks and a *white* dress-shirt with a *red* tie.

"Hi/ p̓, / , I'm / p̓, / Regene / p̓, / Mentrata."

Mentrata spoke with pauses, and after that sentence he said nothing more.

Very to the point.

(no-emotions-on-Mentrata's face)

Jana kept looking at his rugged face with crevices that reflected his age to be about 55 years or more.

His *fading-black* long hair was laced with countless *white* hair.

"Come in please. I'm Jana".

"Let's have a seat at the table."

Both sat *in silence* for a while.

Jana was expecting Mentrata to say something.

...to start the conversation.

Mentrata said nothing.

Mentrata just kept staring.

The *silence* continued.

After 16 seconds of continual silence, Jana decided to speak:

"I know you buried my father...I want to pay my respects to his bones...where is my father?"

Mentrata just stared at Jana.

There was no-indication that he-had-heard-her at all.

Did Mentrata have a hearing problem? Did Mentrata speak English good enough to understand?

"Mentrata is a paralegal in San Francisco, so of course he understood English." Jana reminded herself in her mind.

Mentrata just kept staring.

Then *suddenly* after 25 seconds, there was a visible reaction:

Streams of tears began to come down from Mentrata's *inner-canthi*.

k   a   n   t   h   o   s

In a very deep-and-slow-voice *littered-*with-pauses Mentrata spoke:

"I/ᵖ,/ am sorry/ᵖ,/ for what has/ᵖ,//ᵖ,/ happened... /ᵖ,/ I could not do anything /ᵖ,/ but follow/ᵖ,//ᵖ,/ their orders or/ᵖ,/ I was/ᵖ,/ next!"

The pauses were not   logical
(mathematically speaking)

a b e r r a t i o n s

a b e r r a t i o n s

"As I buried/ᵖ,/ him, I /ᵖ,//ᵖ,/ thought I was /ᵖ,/ going to be next"... /ᵖ,//ᵖ,/

"but they let/ᵖ,/ me go."

"Why/ᵖ,/ did they /ᵖ,/ let /ᵖ,/ me/ᵖ,/ /ᵖ,/ go?..."

... ."I /ᵖ,/ don't know!"

"The body/p̩,/ of /p̩,/ your father is/p̩,/ buried/p̩,/ in the /p̩,/ San Jose /p̩,/ mountains..."

"I will take /p̩,/ you/p̩,/ /p̩,/ there."

"It is an /p̩,/ unmarked /p̩,/ /p̩,/ grave"...

"but I remember /p̩,/ the/p̩,/ large rock/p̩,/ that is near /p̩,/ it". /p̩,/ /p̩,/

"I was/p̩,/ /p̩,/ blindfolded on my/p̩,/ way there/p̩,/ and on/p̩,/ my way/p̩,/ back; but I/p̩,/ was familiar/p̩,/ with the/p̩,/ area/p̩,/ /p̩,/ so I/p̩,/ know where /p̩,/ it/p̩,/ /p̩,/ is".

"I kept/p̩,/ that secret/p̩,/ from those/p̩,/ /p̩,/ /p̩,/ villains."

Mentrata's whole sermon seemed to ramble on *eternally*.

Ramble on ***ETERNALLY!***

Literally!

It was difficult to connect meanings from one word to the next because of all the pauses.

Was this a cultural thing, a speech im*pediment*, or from someone emotionally charged?

Who knows!

S   e   t   s   u   d   a   n

切断

o   w   a   r   i

終わり

The time was *twelve-past-noon.*

Mentrata agreed to show Jana were Wild Feather was buried.

Preparations were made to rent an SUV equipped with GPS and *off-road*-tires.

Jana had lunch with Mentrata in the suite.

Miguel was off doing business errands as they had updated their reunion time.

Mentrata talked about how great her father was in leading a movement to *restore* Hope and Faith for all Native Americans.

Mentrata was younger then Jana's father and her father was his mentor.

"I /ˈp,/have written /ˈp,/two/ˈp,/ books /ˈp,/on what /ˈp,//ˈp,/has happened /ˈp,/and they /ˈp,//ˈp,/will be/ˈp,/ released/ˈp,/ at /ˈp,/my/ˈp,/ passing."

"I want/ˈp,/ to live/ˈp,/ and live/ˈp,//ˈp,/ life/ˈp,/ to the/ˈp,/ fullest/ˈp,/ and be able/ˈp,/ to publish/ˈp,//ˈp,/ these works/ˈp,/ when/ˈp,//ˈp,/ there is no/ˈp,//ˈp,/ /ˈp,/ danger/ˈp,//ˈp,/ to myself. /ˈp,/There is/ˈp,/

another book/ˈp̦/ on this/ˈp̦/ /ˈp̦/ occurrence/ˈp̦/

not complete/ˈp̦/ /ˈp̦/ as of yet. /ˈp̦/"

Jana listened, stared, and responded:

"It is your right to do with your *life* as you please."

Jana continued:

"You are right Mr. Mentrata: life is to be enjoyed. That is something I am learning *to do* every-*day* of my life."

"There are many *hidden secrets* in these *world-societies* we live in."

Jana paused slightly and then continued:

"*Hidden secrets* which I feel are not for the good of what we are trying to accomplish."

"And what we are trying to accomplish is..."

" to live life to the fullest."

" to live life in peace."

" to live life in **true** LOVE."

Jana paused slightly again and then reiterated her perceived obstacles to happiness.

"Hidden Secrets!*"*

Just as Jana was finishing this expression-of-words the hotel suite *door* opened.

Miguel came in and smiled.

He greeted Mentrata and thanked him for *coming.*

There was a mutual affection in the room between all three. It was as if a shared *spirit-of-truth-and-love* embodied and surrounded them.

At *exactly* 1:11 pm: they all made their way to the SUV that was parked downstairs.

Once everyone was in the vehicle, the journey began.

Miguel drove while Mentrata sat in the front passenger seat. Jana sat at the m*id'le* of the back seat to get a clear view of the road ahead of her.

The directions were toward the *Diablo* Range Mountains (that is): the *Devil'*s Range Mountains.

They took Mentrata's *direction* and *headed* toward San Jose on the 101.

From there they took the Alum-Rock-Avenue *exit* and drove past Interstate *6*80 toward Route *1*30 which is now called the Mount Hamilton Road.

The burial location of the murder was *9* miles from Mount Hamilton.

Mentrata had been there at least once a month to the date, after his somewhat recovery (to pay his respects to his *fallen*-friend and as a memorial to one that strived to help others).

As they entered Route 130: Mentrata began to chant in a Native American *language*.

This *startled* both Jana and Miguel who were not expecting it!

When they looked at him: Mentrata had his eyes *close*d and the palms of his hands elevated toward the *sky*.

Jana initially felt uneasy but began to calm herself down.

After a while, Jana *too* closed her eyes and began to chant her own mantra in silence (her chants where in a Native American language different than that of Mentrata).

Jana's use of a Native American language was on an *unconscious* level as she did not understand word-for-word what she chanted but rather sensed its **P***ower!*

Y también *S*in-*Embargo* estas palabras que recitaba en su mente le trajeron una protección poderosa que sintió por dentro.

The chanted *words* of Jana were that of Comanche.

Jana had *heard* THESE *words* at the reservation as a child.

Her great paternal grandmother Mama-Mai would chant THESE *words.*

It always *sooth*ed Jana to hear THESE sounds (*especially* during times when her father would drop her off at the reservation and leave).

As with *any*-young-child: separation from parents is always a difficult experience!

Especially in-the-beginning:(

Miguel was sort of dumbfounded as his approach to life never entailed such supernatural reliance in solving issues.

Miguel was a realist. Miguel was a businessman (starting from a young age).

Miguel never found that connection even as a child. **What** was in front of him is **What** the connection was and **No More.**

Miguel was part of the world and found that planning and executing a well thought-out plan was the proper way toward approaching life issues.

Miguel had relied on **this** frame of mind, **this** mind set, **this** format of thinking all his life.

... a reliable **cognition** especially when everything around him broke-down in front of him.

Something however began **growing** on Miguel since he met Jana.

And **slowly**, still on an unconscious level, **Tinkerings** began aligning themselves to help transform Miguel into a believer and not just one that respected others' beliefs.

These **Tinkerings** were to succeed in the future.

(as its origins were not from this world).

As the SUV continued on its journey, Jana began to see the road with her *eyes-closed*.

This half Irish half Native American woman began to `hover` *high-over* the car as if seeing with *eagle-eyes*.

Jana felt the air around her moving and *shifting*.

Jana *especially* felt her arms *pushing* the air.

Temperature gauging, Jana felt the heat of the sun at a 43-degree-angle above her.

Jana scanned the terrain as if with X-ray scanning:

...everything was *black-and-white*.

11-9-11
9-11-9
9-9-9
11-11-11

Miguel just kept quiet and waited for Mentrata to provide further instructions:

Mentrata had given general directions to the burial site (but not the *exact* directions).

Mentrata needed to be there...to be drawn to the *bones*-of-his-friend.

Energy-pools began to *fluXuate* around Jana as she hovered above: Jana could sense *every-living-creature-that-roamed-those-mountains.*

...from the tallest and heaviest to the smallest and lightest!

Jana could NOT COMPLETELY understand what was *going/\on* in-a-conscious-level.

Jana only knew to give her eternal being the opportunity to take over in areas she knew little of (areas neglected!).

[People! (you yea **you**...reader! AND I!) Let's stop "**neglecting**"!]

Jana did not question her eternal being since she understood more and more the ***cloudment*-state-of-her-human-condition** that enveloped her.

A condition Jana had not as of *yet* completely disconnected from.

Eventually Jana would understand completely.

That moment had not *yet* arrived!

運命

yet!

命運

So Jana just followed her eternal being as if it had always been known (at least in her unconscious-deep-sleep-state!).

After several winding roads Jana began to feel the presence of her father's remains...Jana could feel the DNA call out to her (since her containment was made by the same *strands-of-information*).

(***Butt*** more than that Jana sensed her father's eternal-being.)

Jana glided back to her *body* and opened her eyes and SHOUTED:

"There Miguel!"

"There!"

"to your left/ just past that big rock."

"Please Please pull over!"

Miguel was completely-startled that he jumped slightly from his seat.

With a quick-'cuperation he slowly pulled over.

Mentrata kept his chant in `vocal-motion`.

(keeping his eyes closed.......as if he knew what was going on).

As the car pulled to a **STOP**

Mentrata ceased his chant and opened his eyes.

"She/'p,//'p,/ is /'p,/right, /'p,/ it/'p,/ is /'p,//'p,/here."

"Do you/'p,/ see that/'p,/ opening in /'p,//'p,/the road/'p,/ hidden/'p,/ by the/'p,/ bush?" /'p,//'p,/

"Move/'p,/ in /'p,//'p,/there /'p,/t/'p,/o conceal/'p,/ the/'p,//'p,/ vehicle." /'p,/

Miguel did as instructed.

All of them walked out of the *vehicle* in unison *as-if-they-were-one*!

"Let's /ˈp̩/cross/ˈp̩//ˈp̩/ the /ˈp̩/*high*/ˈp̩/way." /ˈp̩/ /ˈp̩/

They all walked and went toward an opening that could not be seen if one where to just *pass* by.

Only one that *had-known-of-it* could have guessed its location.

And then began the inclination upward.

Miguel had a *pack* on his back in which he carried water and food supplies (along with other essentials in the event that they needed them).

Miguel helped Jana climb the elevations to reach the *plateau* on which the large-rock rested on.

There, in front of the large-rock, stood *three* **16**-inch-diameter-stones together.

Each of those stones had a symbol carved at-its-center.

"There"/ℙ,/

"there/ℙ,//ℙ,/ **He**/ℙ,//ℙ,/is." Mentrata said as he pointed to the three rocks.

Jana began to feel nervous again and began to tremble.

Miguel held her *firmly* but did not say a word as they went *toward* the rocks.

Jana fell to her knees in front of the grave and began to cry:

"father! father! father!"

Jana yelled with tears streaming from her eyes on to-the-*dirt*.

(It was as though Jana *were sanctifying* the site with her tears!)

Suddenly a *gust-of-strong-wind* began to take form and the clouds above began to cover them overhead.

(as if *cooling-the-ground* for their visit [and concealing their presence]!)

Miguel stood beside Jana and began to *tear*-in-his-soul

for Jana.

for her lost.

for the parents he never knew!

The *emotional-an*guish was unbearable.

It was as though a single-*spear*-pierced-everyone present!

The *sting* was unbearable.

The baby within Jana began to move.

Jana could feel the child as she continued to cry uncontrollably.

Little by little, THOUGH, this movement of the child consoled-Jana-*profoundly*.

Jana somehow knew that the child within her would carry her father's entity into *an eternity* to our true home with God Father.

The child was to continue the struggles of this *dirt-world* where their confinements existed (each in different formats).

The "*game*" was not over!

No wars have been won by the enemy!

>Only an i l l u s i o n of a *Win* by those who rule the world!<

Jana qui*et*ly *O*pened-her-eyes.

Jana cleared the P U R E water-*of-tears* around her eyes. As she focused with her eyes, Jana began to see a symbol engraved in each stone.

They had been carved using dirt and wood and muscle!

The symbol on each rock was

a *magnificent* FEATHER

(the symbol of her father).

Jana stood up

turned to her left.

There Jana found *the stick* that had carved each of them!

Jana went over to it

picked it up

then returned to the three rocks.

From the *endpoint* of each feather Jana began to carve a line toward her.

Jana carved and carved, deepening the line to the same dept'*ness* as that of the symbol on each rock.

At the end-of-the-line Jana carved **TWO** WORDS in capital letters on each of the three rocks.

SIX WORDS that took a good while to complete but somehow Jana was able to complete them quickly.

...as if she had the skills of an experienced carver...an experienced sculptor!

Miguel neared to see what Jana had written (as did Mentrata).

As Jana threw the stick to the side (from where she had picked it up from), the *two men* could see the words formed:

"TO ME".

The *two men* did **not** understand what Jana had written.

The *two men* DARED-NOT ask her what the words meant.

Jana knew exactly what the line and the words meant.

"We can go now", Jana spoke *softly*.

Jana went to Mentrata and hugged him.

"*Thank you* for bringing me here."

"…for *not forgetting* my father".

Jana then turned to Miguel and stared at him.

(he stood about 7 feet away).

Jana **raced** toward him and embraced him.

Jana then *whispered* into Miguel's ear:

"I love you my love forever."

"I will love you no matter what!"

Miguel began to TEAR-MORE-HEAVILY this time (as he profoundly embraced his wife).

It was an ***embrace*** SO–PROFOUND that it cannot be described-in-words.

Its LANGUAGE is w o r d - l e s s !

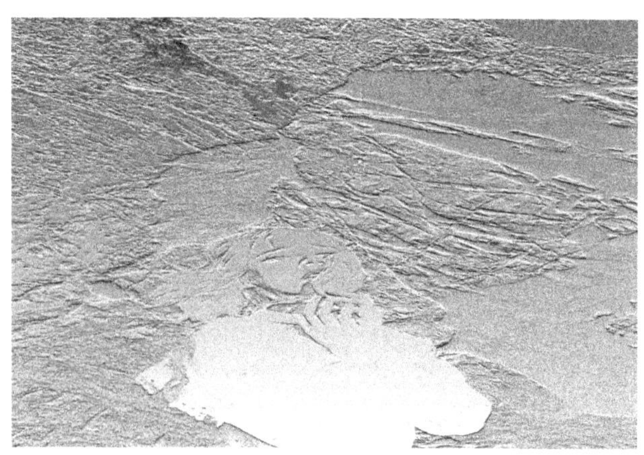

PART **7** of 7

A NEW BEGINNING

J ā n a

Chapter Thirty EIGHT
Prelude to a Continued Life!

Sometimes things don't turn out like you want them...*truth* be said... most times.

Jana had hopes of seeing her father again and spending time with him.

...she desired to create new Earthly moments for those *lost-times* which caused her much **inner-pain** in her father's absence.

Jana, though, did-not-lose-*Hope* or *Faith*.

Jana knew now that her father would always be with her in spirit. This eternal realm which she could *tap* into (**in this world**) if she really brought herself to it.

Jana k*new-now* she was much more than the temporal physical (which is the programmed nature-of-this-world).

Jana kept quiet about her revelations and realizations.

Jana had not shared anything with anyone, except certain aspects with Miguel.

Jana wanted first to get a clear and present grasp of what she had learned and was learning.

It is true that Jana still knew very little.

Yet Jana was beginning to know more as she surrendered her doubts to her eternal self!

Eternal self

Jana understood now that there were (and are) a

Spectrum of non-apparent programmed-forces, controlling eternal beings (misguided energy beings), working alongside the physical rulers of this world to consistently blind the masses from the *truth*, and to blind them from the regular practices of what is *eternal*.

A carefully CONCOCTED series-of-processes with one purpose:

A *Transformation of Energy*.

These "controlling-eternal-beings": wanting to flex a deceitful muscle for the Rebellious Creation: imposing their false deities and consistently promulgating a **worldly** Deity Concept which is non-existence in the realm of eternity.

At the *end* these propagan*doles* have but an *end*.

AN *END*●

With that realization Jana made up her mind to meditate everyday...*seek*ing to find a constant *eternal-connection*.

And, as with anything in this World: *practice* is necessary!

...*b*ecause the body was made-w*e*ak and imperfect...intentiona*l*ly made that way by *i*ts authors to confuse the *e*ternal-being within!...making it a *v*ery easy prey for manipulation and dec*e*it.

Chapter Thirty Nine
Standing Bow: Jana's Writing Project Continues!

In three months' time Jana would give birth to her daughter (or her son) from the love she had shared and was sharing with *Miguel*.

Jana was content.

Jana decided to continue her story...her novel.

Somehow Jana wanted to Mend this character-boy with her father who grew up to be a freedom fighter (irrespective of a world-success-concept).

In Jana's mind, making this story also *represented* her sharing of her Irish ancestry.

The Irish, *natives to their land,* also shared and share in the same struggle for **preservation**... to this day!

Continuing to write the story gave Jana *the essence* of her Irish ancestry she knew little of:

fhios beag:

Mar sin féin, tá an croí ár sinsear *inscríofa* i ngach rud a dhéanaimid!

Agus mar sin tá súil agam a chaomhnú!

Segunda Repetición:

Sin embargo, ¡el corazón de nuestros antepasados *se inscribe* en todo lo que hacemos!

(Y así se conserva la esperanza!)

第三次重複:

但是 / 我們的祖先的心臟是 *落款* / 我們做好/每一件事！

所以希望保留！

תיעיברה הרזחה:

לכב **בותכ** וניתובא בלב, תאז םע
!מישוע וננחנאש רבד

!הרמשנ הווקתה דכו

Cinquième Répétition

(Le nombre de ce monde)
(Le code de cette existence!)

Cependant, le coeur de nos ancêtres **est inscrit dans** tout ce que nous faisons!

Et l'espoir est préservée!

And so:

Jana was enthusiastic about completing her first literary work based on characters derived from her ancestors.

"¿Qué será el continuo?", Jana thought in the language she had acquired for her profession.

Jana pondered *Standing Bow* and his life and his *circumstance*. "¿Qué será el continuo?"

The images ran through Jana's mind as she sat down by her com*put*er.

Images began to form and her question of "¿Qué será el continuo?" ***cease***d.

Jana began to write...

Jana w*rote* and w*rote* and w*rote.*

> The end had seemed very near for
>
> Standing Bow's tribe. Yet, they escaped to
>
> regroup and to continue the struggle for
>
> existence by attempting to repel the
>
> encroaching white man who were aided by

a deceived brethren (other tribes in the vicinity of his breath).

The band of warriors led by Standing Bow raced in the opposite direction of where its home base was...in order to deter the enemy from finding their loved ones. As they rode with great speed, Standing Bow was bleeding from the shoulder; he had been pierced by the enemy's invisible spear...and although he tried to stop it with a leather pack as he rode, the blood continued to flow and Standing Bow fell from the horse.

Immediately, his comrades raced to his aid. They had traveled a good six miles. The day began to dim...turning black.

Standing bow stared at the sky which was

becoming white...he began to lose consciousness. What sustained him from losing the life battle was yelling of voices beckoning him to stay awake...to keep fighting the drowsiness.

His first and second lieutenants continued to apply pressure to his wounds: One from the front shoulder and the other from the back shoulder...as the bullet had gone in and out of his body.

Standing Bow no longer felt pain; and when he tried hard to close his human mind: the *voices* would not let him be.

He kept staring up but saw nothing but white.

Standing bow had survived the physically intense nights.

His comrades had stopped the bleeding.

Days had passed and little by little Standing Bow was restored. Although he was still weak, the teas and foods carefully administered to him made way for his successful recovery.

They were in hiding for over *seven* days when they decided it was safe to return to the tribe.

As they returned...they found no tribe! They began to cry and cry and cry.

Standing Bow was the only one who showed no emotion. He knew the end of their peaceful existence had come to a close...he thought it was the will of the gods and he accepted it.

An end to a "peaceful existence", but not of his people. Standing Bow was determined to fight!

The others however had hopes of reuniting immediately with their loved ones. They wanted to search for their loved ones.

Standing Bow was against any type of immediate search. He knew his men needed to prepare for the battle, and not run blindly and unprepared for the fight.

As a consequence, Standing Bow's army dissolved as mutiny caused by emotional despair took over his men.

After *two* weeks of searching, the deserters driven by despair and other emotions were captured by the white man. They had accidentally run into one of their heavily armed settlements.

Their minds and judgment had been clouded with grief and illusions.

When captured they made no resistance. They had decided that there was no win. Being outnumbered...their hopes had drained from their eyes.

These Comanche men were no longer. Comanche blood no longer vibrated in their veins. They had surrendered it to the white man!

Prior to their search, Standing Bow

attempted to encourage them to fight to the end but intelligently and not in search of loved ones.

In that morning of his plea, they nodded in disagreement and left to begin their search...throwing all hopes of resistance into the air.

And so, Standing Bow was the only one in the band of warriors that kept the flare to fight.

As a result, he escaped into the mountains despite volley after volley of intense invisible spears firing at his direction a few days later.

Not a single bullet of the thousands aimed at him had pierced him. It was as though the Comanche gods protected him!

For what reason was this protection given?

It remains unknown for the moment.

After much contemplation and exploration of the images in her mind, Jana continued to write:

Standing Bow began living in the mountains South West from the plains...they were known as the Tucson mountains.

There he met other warriors that decided not to give up. Rather they took time to *fine tune* their tactics and plan their attack on the white man's settlements.

Although many spoke different languages, they had a common thread...the same enemy from the old world.

They began creating pigeon languages in order to understand each other.

Each warrior had talents and ideas that helped the cause.

Each made truces with their foreign tribe warriors for the benefit of a whole of the original races of the Americas.

Each had information as to where their loved ones may have been taken....and freely shared the information having made a truce amongst themselves.

They also gathered information that not all of their loved ones had been massacred.

These saved ones had been relocated in places called "reservations" which these Native American warriors called "Cetrats" (prisons...as that is what they are.).

Each Native American Warrior understood that the world they knew would never be the same.

Nonetheless they made a determination to continue on by way of a nomadic way (difficult concept for those Native Americans that had lived a sedentary life).

They wanted to continue to live out their cultures and pass them on to their offspring as **unmodified** as possible.

In the band of warriors, women and children were also found. Willing to fight to the end if necessary.

Standing Bow wanted to be with his family, and with the woman he loves.

Regrouping for power was nevertheless his first priority.

This priority was the only way his people were to stand a chance to preserve their way of life.

Standing Bow now knew that no ideal circumstance would ever come to fruition and he was determined to one day reunite with the woman he loves and wed her and love her.

"What is her name?" a woman of the newly formed multi-tribal group had asked him.

"She is **Tlatletla**".

This thin, dark woman from Apache ancestry liked Standing Bow...wanting him as a lover and a corresponding man.

What attracted her most was his quietness and determination.

Yet this woman respected his decision to keep on loving this one woman named **Tlatletla**.

The Apache woman told Standing Bow that she would ask around to this newly formed, independent, multicultural, sparse tribal group to see if they had heard of her and his parents.

Standing Bow did not say a word to her.

Rather, he gave a nod of approval with a

gathering of hands... as a gesture of thank

you.

下 23 人

Tlatletla

Tlatletla was captured and taken to a

reservation in Wyoming.

At the reservation she became aware that

her life as she knew it was gone.

And her Hope and Faith in finding Standing

Bow seemed all but a memory of lost.

About a dozen tribes were represented there. All were forced to stay within the reservation boundaries. The land in which they were imprisoned was inhospitable for growing crop or hunting adequate buffalo. All buffalo had been intentionally slaughtered to end the Native Americans' way of life!

All the captured peoples there seemed to have a long face of defeat; a face that life would never be the same.

The Shamans were no more.

Moreover, all the peoples within each tribe were scattered to prevent an uprising.

All the functional parts of a tribe thus were not intact.

This began a process, little by little, of a killing off of the cultures of the Americas. Cultures that existed before the European invasions. The killings continue to this day!

Genocide had reached the Americas!

It was common practice at that time to remove the Native American children from their homes and take them away to what are now known as "boarding schools".

And so the stripping and slaughter of cultures was in full force.

Having surrendered their arms: the captured were subject to abuse and had to obey whatever came their way.

Tlatletla saw this firsthand and could do nothing to stop this control. Instead, she focused on her escape.

Tlatletla had kept track of the distances she traveled with her jailers. Her objective remained to go out and find her love; even though at times she felt it was hopeless.

Tlatletla's older brothers were also missing as they were separated when they went out to defend the tribe at the time they were captured.

They never returned.

Tlatletla was in constant grievance but tried hard to fight it for it would not bring her closer to any of them.

> The only future that was certain was *uncertainty* itself!
>
> Tlatletla lay quietly in her tent...praying to the gods and trying to find the connection to her love through supernatural means...she felt Standing Bow alive ALIVE!!!
>
> Tlatletla felt him.
>
> As Tlatletla closed her eyes she began to see him and feel him and her pain was abated by those images.

Jana sat on those words in contemplation.

"Tlatletla was slowly winding down to an extinguished light."

"...but the light refused to give in!"

"The light kept its struggle to stay alive!"

Jana had read about boarding schools and how they ruthlessly separated families to break the culture into fragments to be forgotten.

Jana thought,

"They have succeeded."

"Most tribe members, those that survived, now know but fragments of their cultures...attempting in such a LATE PERIOD-IN-TIME to gather remnants of what has become *Points-Of-Extinction.*"

E X TINC TION.

GE NO- 'CIDE.

An Agenda carried out by the ruling class of a fabricated new country in the Americas.

An invading culture valuing itself through a concept of "melting pot" of all cultures.

And this concept was in motion...pressing a propaganda of a fallacious "American" culture at the expense of, and lack of respect for, pre-existing cultures.

The current ruling class' objectives of the United States of America (including those western Europeans countries and the Other installed

Puppet governments in China and elsewhere) remain the same: invading *to-this-day* cultures (and also stripping these cultures of their respective human and natural resources) within its boundaries, along with other cultures (and also stripping these cultures of their respective human and natural resources) in third-world countries that resist a "melting pot" concept of Capitalism (an economic concept of greed, selfishness, propagating disunity amongst groups!...and much much more damage!)

Capitalism

Commercialism

A selfish and self-centered and greedy economic concept meant to divide and consume the masses...Breaking apart families' ways of life in Korea, Vietnam, China, Syria, Lebanon, Iran, Iraq, and all countries in the Americas: including Chile, Guatemala, Panama, Venezuela, Colombia, and the underprivileged masses in the United States of America!

And the list goes on and on.

As Jana's mind wondered away from this critical topic: she closed her eyes.

Jana took a deep breath *in*,

a slow exhale breath *out*,

and Opened her eyes to *the light*,

And then continued her story:

The time was 11 past the full moon. It was time for Tlatletla to make her move. She had no one to join her. All were afraid.

Standing Bow's parents had been murdered in the initial raid on her tribe.

Tlatletla attempted to save them but was knocked to the ground with a blow that secretly jumped up behind her.

During this deadly raid, Tlatletla had lost consciousness and bled slowly from the blow.

But Tlatletla had survived.

"Now is my time", she said to herself and she gathered what she could of water and sacks of meat for her journey.

"I will retrace my steps and find my love!"

As she said these words: tears filled her eyes for she was fighting against unfavorable circumstances.

Nonetheless, Tlatletla moved quickly to regain her integrity.

This Native American slipped like a shadow into the darkness for the moon seemed to be covered by a *shadow*.

Tlatletla felt her way toward the direction she was brought from.

She walked swiftly and breathed at a normal pace to avoid making any noises.

Tlatletla closed her eyes during the

darkness and then opened them when the moon became bright again...helping her see her destination.

Forty days passed and Tlatletla was becoming more and more hopeful because of the amount of terrain she had passed.

Tlatletla felt her body racing to stay alive. She had survived so far by hunting small game and drinking their blood and eating their flesh.

Tlatletla had been thankful to her parents who had taught her the skills to survive in such circumstances.

The time was now late Spring and the

heat of a new and warmer season kept
her alive.

Another 40 days had passed and Tlatletla
was near a river.

Tlatletla stood at the shore of the
river...gazing at the brownish color of the
water streaming by.

She was in contemplation.

After 25 seconds past Tlatletla reached for
water and drank it. It was clean and cool.

It refreshed her.

Tlatletla now possessed a determination
that would not end till she reached her

destination...whenever that was to arrive.

As Tlatletla sat squatted near the water, branches began breaking at a distance.

Tlatletla became startled. She grabbed her spear (a spear she had made of stone and branches), and stood in a warrior alertness stance (even though she had never been in battle as a warrior, she had instincts that prepared her for battle).

From the branches came an enormous huge brown bear. The bear stared at her and began to roar!

Tlatletla was terribly frightened...she quickly initiated options in her mind for an escape. The bear stood at least five feet taller than she.

Since Tlatletla could not swim (for there was never an opportunity of an abundance of water where she could practice), that option was non-existent.

Tlatletla had no way out!

She quickly decided it was better to try to move away from the angry bear and avoid the water at all costs.

Tlatletla knew of bears and that they were swift and powerful.

Tlatletla slowly grabbed her belongings and walked quietly in the direction opposite the flow of water.

The roaring continued...getting louder and louder...prompting Tlatletla to increase her pace.

At that very moment, Tlatletla had Standing Bow in her mind. She wanted to see him again and not leave the Earth without reaching her destination which was her love.

Tlatletla had to be strong even though her entrails were hurting her tremendously...an increasing pain intensifying with every sound that came from the bear.

All of a sudden the bear charged Tlatletla...racing toward her with the sounds of the ground growing louder.

It was as though the gargantuan bear's movements created earthquakes. Tlatletla felt them!

It must be hungry and Tlatletla was its

quencher of hunger.

Tlatletla prepared for battle and stopped running. She could not outrun the bear. She knew that for certain.

Tlatletla stood her ground and began yelling at the beast.

As the beast neared her, Tlatletla knew she could not win the battle.

In milliseconds, the beast became larger and larger.

Tlatletla was determined to fight for her life if that were possible. Her strength came from her determination to see her love one more time.

Tlatletla would not give in easily.

As the beast became a huge monolith, just three feet away from her, Tlatletla felt the chills racing in her abdomen.

What was she to do?!

The bear reached for her with his mouth and then with its right claw.

Tlatletla's body reacted automatically ...swiftly moving in the opposite direction from both enemies: the mouth and the claw!

As the *third enemy* began its descent onto her, Tlatletla raced underneath the bear (between the bear's two legs!). Tlatletla looked like a gopher who races to its hole to go underground.

As the enormous bear began to turn to find its prey, Tlatletla jump at the bear's back and began to climb up quickly!

Tlatletla firmly grabbed its fur as a cub grabs her mother.

Quickly Tlatletla reached the neck of the bear!

The enormous bear became startled and attempted to use its claws to grab that prey behind it; but its limbs were useless.

Moving swiftly to avoid the bear from rolling on the ground, Tlatletla grabbed her knife from behind her belt and attempted to stab the bear at the head.

She was unable to pierce the skull!

Accordingly, Tlatletla immediately raised her speedy hand with the spear and drove the spear through the side of the neck of the beast (repeating this motion for about 16 seconds...she was growing tired.

At the 25th stroke, the bear began to drop to its back in hopes of crushing her prey turned predator.

Sensing the bear's intention, Tlatletla jumped from it and ran as the bear dropped belly up to the ground.

The injured bear attempted to run after Tlatletla.

Instead of being able to stand and run, the bear became paralyzed at the 7th millisecond and stopped moving. It just lay there helpless...slowly bleeding from its multiple inflicted wounds.

Tlatletla ran and ran but could not hear the enemy racing toward her. She turned and saw it immobile on the ground.

Still very cautious and tired, Tlatletla raced to the bushes and hid. From behind the bushes she stared at the giant brown bear. It did not move!

It did not move! Did not move!

Tlatletla sat down and kept staring at it. After about a minute past a quarter hour, the bear remained in the same spot.

Tlatletla decided to go toward it. She felt it had been wounded mortally.

At a distance of seven yards, Tlatletla

stopped.

Then cautiously proceeded forward.

Tlatletla could see that the bear's tongue was out and it seemed to be staring at her...but with a blind stare that could only come from one that has left its own body.

Tlatletla grabbed a nearby rock and threw it at the bear. She wanted to make sure it was no longer occupying that fierce monolithic body that was staring at her.

As the stone struck the bear's nose, it did not move.

It was dead.

Although the bear smelled terrible, Tlatletla decided that she would skin it for its fur and use its flesh for food.

Tlatletla slowly began by first cutting the head off as a whole.

For that task, Tlatletla used a heavy branch which she sharpened with rocks. The tool preparation took about 3 quarters of an hour.

Tlatletla then used this new tool to little by little dismember the vertebrae from the head which consisted of going first through thick layers of skin, fat, and heavy-set muscles.

The last part of this removal required her to use heavy rocks with the tool to separate the most cornerstone bone, ligament, and tendon connecting head and body.

The tool was so well made that the process of dismembering became easy and quick.

In fact, it took longer to create the tool than to dismember the bear's head from its body!

At the complete moment of extraction of the head, huge gushes of blood flowed from that part of the bear's body onto the ground below.

Large birds started closely circling Tlatletla the surgeon.

She waved them away with her spear.

The large birds then circled high above the carcass hoping to steal some or all of the spoils!

Unable to maneuver for a quick steal, the birds calmed themselves down and settled into a patience in nearby rocks.

The Large Flyers conceded their inability to safely act on their natural frenzy itches.

And so the birds' tactic changed.

Tlatletla then proceeded to dismember, one by one, each of the bear's legs from their joints.

Tlatletla was careful not to cut herself with the bear's razor-sharp claws!

Once this task was complete, Tlatletla proceeded to the next task.

Tlatletla carefully began skinning the bear beginning from the five points she had prepared on the bear's core.

By the time Tlatletla started this task, the bear's corpse was sufficiently stiff like a trunk of a tree.

Once she skinned the bear's sky-exposed parts, Tlatletla used rocks and a thick branch to get leverage to role the beast over to begin to finish the skinning.

As Tlatletla attempted do this, one large bird, from the bird committee standing on the nearby rocks, swooped by seeking to grab some bear flesh.

Tlatletla immediately threw a rock at it, missing it.

Tlatletla had collected a pile of rocks just for the probable task of warding off those hungry birds.

The bird did not return after that attack, and the other five just stood high in the distance. Waiting.

Finally, Tlatletla washed the fur in the river and set it up to dry in the sun. This fur would come in handy for the winter.

The whole process took about 4 and a half hours.

Tlatletla felt happy at her unintentional unexpected catch!

Tlatletla cut up the bare bear corpse into precise cuts for future use which took an additional two hours to complete.

Then Tlatletla carefully cut the meat into

strips to make jerky of this bear's flesh. The amount she decided to take was the amount she could comfortably carry or drag with her.

After gathering together the meat into a large pile, Tlatletla took this manageable catch 1600 feet away from the rest of the corpse (which consisted mostly of bone and lard).

She separated herself from the bones of the beast in order to avoid problems during the night with coyotes and other night predators.

After Tlatletla was at a good distance from the bones and the rest of the corpse, the first predators were of course the waiting committee of Large Birds.

Their patience had paid off and they feasted as much as they could possibly consume.

These flying predators then went to nearby rocks and slept with their stomachs fully satisfied.

All the whiles, Tlatletla washed up and prepared her camp for the night.

In the morning Tlatletla began drying the meat by placing them on racks she made from sticks.

As the meat strips dried, she went to the river to refresh herself.

Later Tlatletla better prepared her camp for the duration of her stay.

After 7 days' vigilance of allowing the meat to dry, Tlatletla started her journey in search of her love.

Tlatletla began walking alongside the river with all of her belongings, and dragging three large packages of jerky bear meat!

The rest of the meat Tlatletla could not carry, because of the weight, she carefully sealed and buried it.

If she ever returned to that spot, she would know where the food was.

Alternatively, she left a sign indicating food underneath in the event any person who happened to pass by can access if there was a need.

Chapter Forty
Dawning Change

Miguel had introduced into the world's baked goods menu an *uusi* way of looking at the needs of the DAMAK TADINIZI .

Many of these introduced goods were completely unique and Miguel had patented their recipe and shape in order to hold a solid growth for this corporation (which had started out as a sole-proprietorship decades past).

These baked goods were now one of seven corporations, owned and operated by Miguel, that manufactured or distributed products that included baked goods, electronic hardware components for a variety of electronic devices, household and business furniture made from oak wood with original design, and software applications for hardware computers. For this last mentioned product line, Miguel had brought in computer and programming engineers in addition to other vital personnel.

On occasion, Miguel would bring home some of the pastries to Jana from his baked goods corporation.

Jana was now almost 2nd to the last month of her pregnancy. She had visibly swollen up to a mature state of pregnancy.

Jana began feeling cramps in her legs as she made her daily morning walks along the strand.

The doctor had prescribed her additional iron and calcium tablets. Jana did not want to take these supplements. However, she followed the doctor's recommendations due to the evident appearance of skin tissue loss around the buds of her fingers and increased cramps.

And, Jana, for the first time, began regular conversations with her mother over the phone.

These new phone sessions were something rare in the past, but becoming more regular in the present.

Both women were eager to see the child and grandchild. Both worked at finding names they liked for either the girl or the boy that was to come!

Miguel was making preparations to allow his responsible and competent managers (who cared as much as he did about his growth vision for his goods) to take over large parts of the administrative responsibilities that he had at the beginning to the present.

Miguel needed to free up time.

Miguel needed to slow down.

Miguel wanted to make time for Jana, and the baby that was on its way.

Jana's trust in Miguel had grown such that she had made preparations to donate all of her furniture in her apartment to the local thrift stores, and to give up her apartment at the south west corner of Ocean Park and Euclid Street by the end of the current month.

Jana was completely certain of her decision (a decision that made Miguel feel happy that she was letting go of her past and trusting in a future with him and their child!).

Hooooray!:)

Two weeks past and Jana went to the doctor for a general check-up. The doctor had confirmed that the baby would be born in about 2 months!

Miguel was present in hearing the good news!:) He wanted to participate as much as possible in Jana's pregnancy.

"¡Que hermoso va ser nuestro hijo!", Jana whispered into Miguel's ear after giving him a gentle kiss.

As Jana breathed: she breathed in happiness.

Jana thought, "Truly this is the blissfulness of a union between two people told in *romance* stories!"

"..only better!!!…it has **materialized** for me and for Miguel!"

"A reality now more than just images in my mind…something that has become a true inspired *presence* of the present!!!!!!!"

At noon the following day, Jana was thoroughly inspired to continue writing her novel. She sat down, prepared the computer, closed her eyes momentarily, took a deep breath, and began to write `with` her hands as to what she saw `with` her mind!:

The night had been peaceful for Tlatletla. She slept in peace. Tlatletla had survived an attack...and she had been fed!!!!!!!

Her legs had strengthened considerably considering the extra load of supplies she had acquired.

Tlatletla had become more fit now from her journey than when she had started.

She felt at peace in knowing that she was on her way to her Hope's destination, to her Faith's destination.

Tlatletla continued her journey early that morning.

After walking a good 16 kilometers, Tlatletla came to a crossing that led to a prairie.

Tlatletla recognized that location as the outermost outskirts from where her tribe came from.

It was the location from where the sun descended.

Tlatletla's tribe originated from the opposite direction to that location in the plains where the sun ascended.

With that acquired orientation, Tlatletla then advanced an additional 16 kilometers.

As it was becoming dark and since she was becoming tired, Tlatletla set up camp and built herself a fire.

As midnight rolled through, Tlatletla slept beautifully: hidden beneath her tipi; wrapped around the bear that had sought her demise.

Tlatletla smiled in her dream!

At about 4 a.m., a noise that rustled the dry grass woke her; it was at a distance...she could hear its advance.

Concerned, Tlatletla disinclinedly walked out of her blanket comfort and into the cold tipi and then out into the colder outside.

With her left hand firmly grasping her spear, Tlatletla was ready for a fight.

It was completely dark outside as the moon

had gone away, and the sun was yet to commence its daily dance.

Tlatletla relied rather on scent and sound more than on sight.

As Tlatletla walked she neared the ground to hear better any possible advancement of the intruding sound.

Tlatletla listened intently.

After a good while of listening, Tlatletla heard nothing.

The temperatures were too cold to stay outside standing, Tlatletla decided to take the risk and return to the tipi and to the bear fur.

After warming herself sufficiently, Tlatletla

continued to listen intently.

Her tiredness and the warmth of the fur began to take her into her dreams...and into a dream Tlatletla went:

Tlatletla began to roam in her dream near an unknown river...she somehow went into it and began to do something she had never done before:

swim!

The deep water Tlatletla bathed in was warm and the fluidity of the water began to caress her gently.

To Tlatletla , the water had become beautiful hands that provided affection to her...the sort of affection she had sought from a man: the man she loved...Standing

Bow.

Tlatletla felt kisses and hugs and touches to her sexual parts that had been asleep within her up to now!

The fondlings intensified and Tlatletla began to feel a growing orgasm.

Tlatletla moaned with passion...feeling the hands of Standing Bow inside her.

It felt so powerful that her moans intensified to a climatic orgasm...at that moment Tlatletla burst out a scream of satisfaction from within and from out of her dream!

When Tlatletla "came" she awoke from her sleep in a peaceful state as if the dream and her wake state had become one!

Tlatletla was calm and breathing in the experience of delight.

After breathing with her eyes closed for a good while, Tlatletla felt beneath her clothing and noticed that she was completely wet in and around her vagina.

Tlatletla lay there without a fear in the world.

As daylight began, Tlatletla walked out of the tipi and took in the cold air.

The cold air cleansed her lungs...preparing them for the day!

The coldness had become her friend again as it was slowly churning the air into a warmer state (in collaboration with the sun).

After packing most of her belongings on that continuing day, Tlatletla went to a nearby water hole and wash up her body in the 52-degree Fahrenheit water!

Tlatletla then proceeded to continue to walk toward her love somewhere in the East.

It was midday and Tlatletla smiled at the sky: receiving the warmth from the sun that had kept her body sound all of her life.

Tlatletla was grateful for the elements the gods had provided her and her family: in good times and in difficult times.

Tlatletla was aware that change was inevitable as life reels circularly to a beginning and an end and then to a cycle of speed which became an eternal existence to a peace.

After seven hours of walking without a halt, Tlatletla reached her tribe's last known encampment.

That encampment was part of a cycle of locations her tribe took for generations...a cycle governed by food supply needs and seasonal changes in weather.

Tlatletla found nothing there but the wind blowing over what was once her home.

Everything Tlatletla knew was now but a memory.

Tlatletla found no one; not a single human was within her vision's distance!

What was Tlatletla to do?

She felt a despair growing within her...an anguish began to set in deeply.

Tlatletla forced herself to take control of her emotions.

She literally forced herself!

"**No**", she said to the body which was her prison in a world that was not her own.

"You will not bring me down! You will obey me!", Tlatletla yelled to the winds...directing her determination and stubbornness to the "warden" who kept her locked in this prison called the body and the environment....a combination built for reasons unknown, or not at all clear.

Tlatletla closed her eyes and took a deep

long breath.

She squatted for a good while, then, at the seventh ring of her ears, Tlatletla slowly stood and proclaimed:

"If not in this prison life then in eternity we will be Standing Bow!"

"If not in this prison life then in eternity we will be Standing Bow!"

"If not in this prison life then in eternity we will be Standing Bow!"

After repeating her determined and fully endorsed conviction, Tlatletla immediately felt an eternal peace take hold of her...bringing all the fragmented energies of her body into one of peace.

> Tlatletla's eternal mind had captured the essence of her true self... her eternal self...that eternal entity that has no beginning nor an end.

Jana felt a jolt within her and stopped typing.

It seemed the baby was telling her, "I am here!".

Jana smiled.

"I am waiting for you my love; to see you; to hold you; to love you; to introduce you to your father".

Chapter Forty One
Mexico City

Miguel had to fly to Mexico City for a restructuring meeting of one his Mexican based companies.

He let Jana know that he was going to be absent for a week.

In her mind Jana knew that she must go…to see his place of origin; to lend him support; to be with him!

To be with him!!!! Jana felt that need.

"I would like to be with you on this trip", Jana told Miguel.

"Do you think that coming with me on this business trip is wise my love?...you are far along in your pregnancy."

Jana looked Miguel straight into his eyes, held his hands with hers, and said:

"I want to be there with you...to see your origins, to meet your friends, to lend you support...but only if that is okay with you."

Miguel looked at Jana in silence.

After a while he neared himself to her and said:

"You are always welcomed to join me wherever I go. I am here for you always."

Silence fell.

A moment of vibrations began.

Their lips met, their breathings touched one another's inhalation.

Then began a gentle kiss.

And then another.

And then another:)

[Oh my the fires are still burning!:) Hooray!:)]

The series-of-kisses were followed by a joining of forehead to cheek, side by side.

Both seeking to mend themselves into one.

Both seeking in combining one-energy from two bodies.

Slowly they closed each other's eyes with an inhalation.

And then both felt their energies become One.

Two minds intertwined into eternal vibrations of One!

A plural of a One.

Plurality became One!

It seemed as though *time* had stopped.

Or disappeared for that matter.

That restrictive-mechanism collapsed if only for that moment!

M ^L $\Rightarrow$ ^ G (-^M) ∃ 7A^{-1} ∞∀□, ¬ the bodies in which they were encased, imprisoned, brought them back to it.

[There was no escaping the confinement while they remained in them.]

[Only Jesus Christ Accomplished That!]

[And after escaping those confines it is not over for most still!.......it is still a process-to-freedom away from the mess-of-the-Creation!]

When both Jana and Miguel opened their eyes, they were in sync!

J⇔M

∀∃ dy/dx $^{\pi}$ ¬lim f(n) □
         n→ c

...as if they realized something beyond the hidden.

There were no words exchanged (everything was just known as if the same-programming-chip had been placed in them both).

Their minds were in sync at that very moment!

After that odd yet unusually familiar experience, both love birds prepared for their flight to Mexico.

Miguel and Jana were scheduled to leave California *Sun*day at 4:30 a.m.

The day was *Thur*sday and Jana had some time to continue her writing.

Jana was excited about the trip!

Memories as a student in Mexico City brought Jana much excitement back then.

And now the idea of going back to this beautiful nation rekindled that excitement!

Mexico City…the vibrant-bustling-city-of-many-colors!.

Mexico City…the land of enchantment and passion! uuh-la-la:)

The morning of 13 April 2008 was a vibrant one....the airs were cleared of clouds as if it were settled that the flight to México City would be a pleasant one...allowing a good view of Mexico's landscape.

Miguel had booked two first class tickets near the window that faced *west*. He had also booked an additional four seats around theirs so that they would have plenty of ample space to be away from others.

Miguel wanted it to be special.

He had booked with Méxicana Airlines.

Originally, he had planned on chartering a private jet. But, Miguel cancelled that idea deciding that it would be best to help this airline which was going through financial difficulty.

His loyalty to México and its businesses was firm.

"Divided we fall", Miguel had told himself on making his final travel plan decision to go through this struggling airline instead.

Jana had slept well the night before.

She had packed all her necessities and those of Miguel's 2-days before the flight, on Friday.

The flight to Mexico was pleasant as Miguel described the Mexican landscape from the air...all the rigid mountainous terrain and towns and cities that they passed.

All can be seen from high altitude!

When they landed in México City, a limousine was waiting for them. The driver began to drive both Miguel and Jana to one of Miguel's houses at the outskirts of the Big City.

This particular home had seven bedrooms with seven bathrooms. On the property was a rectangular pool for laps, and a Jacuzzi, along with a four-car garage and a large green lawn.

On the 5 acre property there also existed a medium size cottage house reserved for the property-keeper and her family.

Jana was not aware of this house and was excited to see it.

As Miguel and Jana were driven by the chauffer through a south one-way highway, they held each other lovingly: thinking of the immediate moments-of-happiness they had been sharing.

The limousine was comfortably driving at 70 miles an hour. The sky had become cloudy as if it wanted to rain. Their love was all the sunshine both Jana and Miguel needed at that moment.

Suddenly, the unthinkable was upon them.

A loud commotion began happening immediately in front of them...so much so that it caught Jana's and Miguel's attention.

Loud noises began intensifying in volume, accompanied by increasing rumbling movements from underneath the stretched vehicle.

In less than 4.3 seconds: a WALL of mounting cars began to form in front of the limousine: creating a massive smoking WALL!

The driver placed his foot **hard** on the break hoping to stop the limo's momentum toward this sudden WALL!

The *l-o-n-g*-car simply skidded at-the-same speed of 70 miles per hour on the wet asphalt...UNable to sto^P!

Jana knew this was the end of what they've known to this point in this 𝕽ealm of existence.

Jana grasped Miguel's hand and held him: whispering in his ear...

"Forever I am with you my love".

In that instant, the limousine collided with the wall of cars.

Jana felt herself become free of her body and rose-with-POWER: breathing in the energies around her...consuming them and keeping them safe for their journey home.

Shesha was able to see without human eyes again and saw Miguel's spirit drifting toward the Second Source's waiting area.

...a place prepared for the completion of the consumption of the energy that began with the capture into carbon-based organisms...the conversion/transformation was about to be complete...ready for consumption by $\mathfrak{R}$a!

But Jana (Shesha) intervened!

Jana (Shesha) grabbed Miguel and brought him $\dot{i}n_tO$ herself, "We **now are** One together my love. We **are now** One!"

Miguel's energy smiled...beginning to understand what was *micro-transpiring* in-him.

Miguel was not a "he" anymore but an "it"!: A being returning to its true nature: even if in a weakened-*manipula*ted state...jostled-by-all-the-deceptions-and-*manipula*tions-of-the-5th *dimension.*

*Manipula*tion!

Irrespective, Miguel was now safe of the mal attempts at his soul by the evil one.

As where the other souls Jana (Shesha) had acquired within herself.

Jana had the choice to burst from the confines of this planet and the rest-of-Creation and return back home: but she (Shesha) knew the war was not over as of yet.

And so

And so

Ando So!!

Shesha prepared to remain in the 5th *dimension* until the calling was made by the chief-administrator.

This chief-entity, Jesus Christ, was charged with ending Creation by bringing all dispersed energies to return (by filtration) to the Source (*our-One-true-Home*).

At the calling of the Father in Heaven, Jesus Christ was ready to end the 𝕽ebellion completely.

As her great-grandmother had done before her (which was herself): Jana would remain to protect the energies from going easily into the 𝕾econd 𝕾ource's planned agenda.

In fact, Jana was a manifestation-of-Shesha thrown back into a carbon after a struggle she had with 6-million minions-of-the- dark-*light* in the battle of Broken-Arrows!

satellitibus in lucem

Back into the accident suffered by Jana and Miguel, and the multiple peoples on this southward Mexican highway, the scenes were atrocious to view.

The human rescue workers moved quickly to remove the baby in the empty-corpse of Jana...performing a c-section.

When they reached the child: the child was alive!

Alive became evident when a rescue worker named Benedetta Carlini performed the c-section (being a nurse for 34 years) against the advice of the lead rescuer who said that the baby was probably dead.

"DEAD NOT!"

Yelled **Benedetta Carlini** and immediately performed the operation....removing life-from-death!

This child of Jana's and Miguel's, a male born under death and extracted to life via an emergency C-section, would one day

Take Back what the **Second Source** had consumed, and then help destroy what **It Created**.

...and by so doing, completely destroying the enemy's will and bringing its energy through-the-refinement...sifted and its elements divided, back into the realm before Creation...Into the realm of the **First Source**: our home!

Chapter Forty Two
A New Child!

And indeed the child survived!

He was named **Mi'Kha-el**.

Mi'Kha-el was taken to Oklahoma to be brought up by his grandmother.

Mi'Kha-el would grow up to become a resistance-to-the-norm which blinded-the-people and the rest of the Carbons!

And upon this child's Carbon-death: **All End** would come upon **C**reation, as Jesus Christ would return to claim an end to all evil.

As an instrument, This Child was destined to forcefully wield away the final sweep of the **S**econd **S**ource's power of deception and consumption and accumulated GROWTH!

 And indeed Hope and Faith [The Merris] was given to the energies confined in their prison: the Carbons including the humans!

碳沒有更多

الكلربونون ال أككثر

άνθρακες όχι περισσότερο

The de-evolution tactics of the enemy are being closed.

The de-evolution tactics of the evil spirit that invades the human encasement is NOT allowed to continue further! God Father is ending the rebellion in increments of shorter frequencies! (Thank God!).

Chapter Forty Three (7)

You!

The Reader…
Have Hope!
Have Faith!
Awaken!
Take Courage!

Stand Firm!

Amén.

God is with you.

You

[End of Book 3 of 3 of Jana Trilogy Novel]

--- --- -

<u>Message from Mi'Kha-el Feeza:</u>

Mi'Kha-el Feeza WEBSITE:

Eternoi.Com

Buenos Días Reader!

Regeneration of Love and Resistance for the common good is
working at my website. We are looking for like-minded
individuals and organizations to collectively help rid ourselves
of the ills of our communities in this world peacefully.

We seek to bring the betterment of the common good to the
forefront of the consciousness of every single human being,
A.I., and extraterrestrial. And in so doing, bring fruitful,
constructive change, peacefully, to all of the world's and
Earth's inhabitants for the benefit of all as a whole!

If you'd like to join one of our committees for the
Regeneration of Love and Resistance…come visit and join!:)
The more free minds the better! Together we are a Collective
Mind that is bringing change to the world and the Earth for the
betterment of the common good! We are Eternoi
Humanitarian Organization (Eternoi).

We, Eternoi, believe there is a good fruitful solution to every
ill in this world and on this planet! God gave us a mind to
think! Let's use it for the common good! We are wholly
Volunteer Based. We never collect any monies directly into
the organization as a whole. Any expenses to promote an
Eternoi solution to a world ill are paid by each member, as to

each member's own will and ability, directly to the service provider, vendor, etc. Example of expenses includes assembly permit fees, etc. Consequently and by design, every member of Eternoi is a volunteer, including the leadership. We, Eternoi, never solicit expense monies from anyone OUT OF the Eternoi membership body. Specific committees are involved in seeing which members are willing and able to help pay the Eternoi solution expenses, as described, directly to the service provider, etc.

And, Eternoi membership is always FREE. One becomes an Eternoi member after being successfully vetted to a specific committee. We believe in the goodness of every single human being. We believe that change for the betterment of the common good comes by example, encouragement, and by awareness!

Have Faith and have Hope and move forward in love!

May God the Father, who is in Heaven and within us, bless you always!

Sincerely,

Mi'Kha-el Feeza
eternoi@protonmail.com

This novel is also dedicated to
God The Father
The Only God
The Only Joy
Faithful, Loving, Nurturing

Amén

"Moses and Aaron then went into the Tent of Meeting. When they came out, they blessed the people; and the glory of the Lord appeared to all the people."

"Fire came out from the presence of the Lord and consumed the burnt offering and the fat portions on the altar."

"And when all the people saw it, they shouted for joy and fell facedown."

Leviticus
9:23-24

ACKNOWLEDGEMENTS AND NOTES

All final output Images in the novel by the author. All Artwork in the novel by the author. All final versions images found in the novel created by the author. Origins of some raw images used as a base for artwork by the author originating from elsewhere in their raw original format noted below.

Only Raw Free Use Images (from pexels.com, pixaybay.com, et al.) or Raw Pubic Domain images used from their original format into the author's artwork where used in the novel, where final artwork arrangements of images where made by the author. All other images in the novel produced exclusively by the author.

The author would like to thank and acknowledge the following people for their contributions in preparing the novel for publication:

Craig Longshore from the Oklahoma Forestry Services at Sallisaw in 2015, Friday, October 5th. Thank you Mr. Longshore for your willingly professional and very friendly and helpful assistance in providing the author with vital data as to the most common native tree species found in the Muskogee County area.

The author would like to thank ALL THE MODELS found in the final artistic art format photographs produced by the author in this novel for presenting their God given bodily images willingly. ¡Gracias! ...y que Dios santísimo siga bendiciéndolos en donde se encuentren... ¡en ésta o la próxima vida!

Finally, thank you to these photographers for their free use original images used in the artwork by the author in this novel: Gerhard G; Sipa; Marcel Langthim; Thomas G; Cottonbro; Warren K Leffler; Polina Tankilevitch, Andrew; Ottoni Lu Ottoni; Andrea Piacquadio; Alvin C. Kraenzlein; H.Hach; Dan Evans; Andi Ravsanjani Gusma; Anete Lusi; Elijah O'Donnell; Luiz Fernando; Julia Volk; Rodnae Productions; Sam Lion; Hamed Almari; Quintin Gellar; Hassan Ouajbir; Ba Tik; Eunhyuk Ahn; David Mark; Armin Rimoldi; Artem Beliaikin; Victoria Boirodinova; Zorro Zombie; Heyn & Matzen image of Joseph Two Bulls; Erika Wittlieb; Ian Beckley; Miriam Espacio; Min An; João Cabral; Edward S. Curtis Piegan; John Vachon; Timothy H. O'Sullivan; Zinpix; Yan Krukov; Neto Soares; David De Giovanni;Alexander Krivitskiy; Bhargava Marripati; Raul Juarez; Ricardo Esquivel; Andreza Vasconcelos; Burak Fatih;Jonathan Borba; Katerina Holmes; Kathryn Archibald; Daria Shevtsova; Ketut Subiyanto; Matheus Bertelli; Meru Bi; Pavel Danilyuk; Anna Shvets; Tatiana Twinslol; Mateus Souza; and a thank you to the Brazilian National Archives; and Fenno Jacobs. ¡Gracias!

And thank you readers for taking the time to read something different!...and hopefully something that will help transform your lives to serve your community better, and to find contentment in small actions for a better world!

Sincerely,

Mi'Kha-el Feeza

About The Author

No. The Author is not Full of Shit! [Well: maybe sometimes, temporarily, after eating:)]

The author is from Santa Monica, California. He is (among many things like most of us) a musician, visual artist, and literary writer. This may be his very first and very last writings in terms of "a novel" for many reasons that go beyond his control.

Mi'Kha-el Feeza is a graduate from the University of California, Los Angeles with a degree in history. He is also a graduate from Loyola Marymount University, Los Angeles with a master degree in education. Mi'Kha-el Feeza attended under an assumed name!

The author wishes to evidently EXPRESS his *will* to help every-single-human-being to be awaken from the deceptions of this world and conformity thereof (controlled by those in power who control all sources of communication) so that he and she may find *their true nature* AWAY FROM the prison bodies and world "we" are contained in: A world inhabited by entities forced into Carbon encasements for the *ultimate* purpose of extraction of one's energy.

Wishing you a wonderful day filled with complete Peace and Contentment as you successfully attain your *true nature* that existed BEFORE THE CREATION of-this-world:)

oT eht stsinataS taht elur eht dlrow: potS gniyalp sa fi sretsefinam-fo-a-enod-laed. oN slaed evah neeb deifidilos; on sraw evah neeb now. oN egaugnal detaerc lliw reted na-dne-ot-ruoy-emag. cigaM dna sllepS era sloot fo a naicigam...a tcudorp fo eslaf sesimorp...a gniralf thgil gnimoc ot sti elzzif!

elzzif elzzif elzzif

tahW si fo nam? *tahW si fo* nuS? *tahW si fo* lasrevinU yrotirreT?: a mroftalp tuohtiw elbats dnuorg!

...A gnihsem fo seigrene ot eb ylenif desuffid dna denethgiarts rof gnissecorp kcab ot rieht *nigiro*....gnisol lla lortnoc fo noilleber.

noilleber: ylleb pu!

ehT seirotcaf era gnimoc ot a esolc...lla stnemele gnieb nekater rof *eht-gnisolc-fo-eht-rood!*

ecnO eht rooD'si tuhS...

...ereht si oN-nruteR

osergeron

Jesus Christ is the Only Way to True Salvation!

J

Jana was written by the author from 2007 to 2018, with final editorial revisions from 2019 to November 2020 (13 years of writing to complete) in the following locations:

- Harvey Bay, Queensland, Australia
- Santa Monica, California
- Malibu, California
- San Diego, California
- San Francisco, California
- Oahu, Hawaii
- Kauai, Hawaii
- Pacific Ocean, 700 miles from Kona on a Hawaiian Airlines Aircraft
- Tulsa, Oklahoma
- Tucson, Arizona
- Grand Junction, Colorado
- Baltimore, Maryland
- "Agantao" The Tin Can [my exile]
- Strange Town
- Crenshaw/Coliseum Streets in LA
- The Lazy Living Room: Larchmont Village

...villagers [these and the like around the world] you are allowed to Awaken! Look around you, breathe, and see beyond your own comforts! Yes villagers: others exist that need your help! ¡Vámonos! True Help Not Crumbs. Need an Incentive: By Helping Others You Help Yourselves! J

- City of Bell (one hour afternoon)
- Seattle, Washington
- Whittier, California

9 781955 535687